Black
Fox
of
Lorne

Books by Marguerite de Angeli

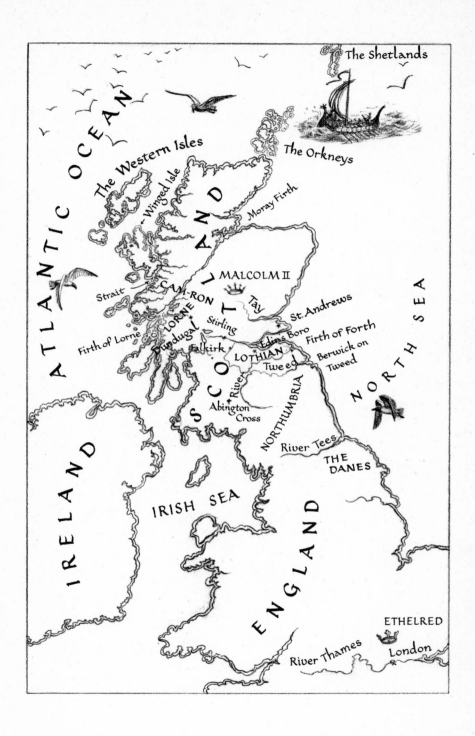

The Shetlands

ATLANTIC OCEAN

The Western Isles

The Orkneys

Winged Isle

SCOTLAND

Moray Firth

MALCOLM II

Strait

CAM-RON

Tay

St. Andrews

NORTH SEA

LORNE

Stirling

Firth of Lorne

Dundugal

Falkirk

Edins Boro

Firth of Forth

LOTHIAN

Berwick on Tweed

River Tweed

Abington Cross

NORTHUMBRIA

IRELAND

River Tees

THE DANES

IRISH SEA

ENGLAND

ETHELRED

River Thames

London

Where the
storm began

NORWAY

Holding above
the Fiord

Black Fox
of Lorne

MARGUERITE DE ANGELI

JUTLAND

The Jeweled Talisman of
HARALD REDBEARD

To the
Frankish
Country

DOUBLEDAY & COMPANY, INC., GARDEN CITY, NEW YORK 1956

LIBRARY OF CONGRESS CATALOG CARD NO. 56-8233

COPYRIGHT ©, 1956, BY MARGUERITE DE ANGELI
LITHOGRAPHED IN THE UNITED STATES OF AMERICA
ALL RIGHTS RESERVED ·
DESIGNED BY ALMA REESE CARDI

*This book is dedicated to my dear friend and
editor, Margaret Lesser, and to the other members of
Doubleday Junior Books, with grateful affection.*

M. DE A.

I saw a stranger yestere'en;
I put food in the eating place,
Drink in the drinking place,
Music in the listening place;
And in the sacred name of the Triune
He blessed myself and my house
My cattle and my dear ones.
And the lark said in her song,
  Often, often, often,
Goes Christ in the stranger's guise.
  Often, often, often,
Goes Christ in the stranger's guise.

OLD GAELIC
RUNE OF HOSPITALITY
FOUND BY KENNETH MACLEOD
  COPIED BY ME FROM BOOK
  IN SKEABOST HOUSE, SKYE

Marguerite de Angeli
JUNE 1954

1 Brus rose when he heard his father's voice, and left the kid he was skinning, telling Thorfinn the thrall he would be back. He slipped out the door, ran up the rise through the trees to another work shed where Jan, his brother, was bent over a task he loved, carving pictured letters called runes. The task had really been set for Brus.

Jan looked up.

"Quick," said Brus, "Give place. Our father comes. I could hear his voice complaining to Mother loudly, and when he came near the work shed I left quickly, for you are supposed to be there and I here. Thorfinn thinks you have been there this long while, but our father might guess it was I if he saw me. He knows how little you like kid-skinning and he knows how rune letters will not form for me. Quick! Run!"

Jan had already risen to let Brus sit in his place. He was used to hearing this voice, so like his own, in secret speech and secret plotting, for they were twins, so like in voice and look, in manner and motion, that one was easily mistaken for the other. The game was a part of their lives. They could always trick the servants; often they could trick their father, but it was not easy to deceive their mother, though she, too, sometimes called one by the other's name.

Now Jan wondered what was afoot.

"Is our father brave with new ale?" he questioned.

"No, it seems not," said Brus, shaking his head. "There has been a dispute about the land. Our father's brothers, Agnar and Nils, have taken back the high field where always our milch cows have been. 'Tis not only that. They have taken, too, the right to the forest where each year we got our firewood. Harken!"

But who could help hearing that bellow?

"What place is there for foster sons?" their father roared. "Now this field, that forest, now that stream, this hunting place! The holding above the fiord is not enough for so many." He spoke to Ragnhild, his wife, as if it were she who had been at fault. "The families of my elder brothers crowd the land. In summer, when the gods draw new grass from the earth, their cattle are as grasses themselves for number. There is not room for all."

Ragnhild held her peace as always when her lord was speaking. He went on.

"I, Harald Redbeard, must look elsewhere for my living; I, because I am a foster son of my father and not inheritance-born. Already I have sent forth two sons from the home place with Gudmond the Bold. They have never returned. It may be they have found a home. It may be they sleep in the sea-god's palace beneath the waves. Who knows?"

Jan and Brus could now see their father and mother standing with sad looks as they spoke of the brothers who had not come back from a-Viking.

"But we have left to us our twin sons, Brus and Jan. They are grown tall and strong and handle well the bow and short sword, the tiller and the oar. Now we shall go a-Viking. The lands of Britain are in easy reach and soft. Your kinsman, Heming the Dane, as you know, already has made settlement there. He will welcome us. The earth is good and the airs are gentle. There we shall go. I make ready the ships. See you to the housegear and food. I shall talk to the men and thralls, for they are sworn to follow me."

He stalked off toward the stable, then called back to Ragnhild. "I go now to my elder brother's to talk of this matter. But first I shall speak to the housecarls and thralls."

Brus and Jan looked into each other's eyes, speaking together as often they did, "A-Viking! We are now men. We go a-Viking!"

The farm or holding where Brus and Jan lived, above the fiord, was in Norway near the southern coast, within easy reach of Danish country, whence their mother had come, and near to the lands of their father's foster brothers. Harald their father, had been adopted by their grandfather when he was ten, and his own father and mother had been lost at sea. He could inherit land of his foster father only by consent of those "inheritance-born."

Brus and Jan, like all boys of good family in this early time, a thousand years ago, were required to learn all manner of skills. They must learn to carve letters on a rune stick. How else might they leave messages or record events? They must learn the art of poetry, so necessary for the remembrance of the deeds of heroes to be told in sagas. For the rhythm of poetry helps remembrance. They must learn the laws of the land so they could take their places at the gathering where all people of the district met each year to settle disputes, to sentence those who had broken laws, to hear news exchanged and sagas sung, to test their strength in games and wrestling. They must learn draughts and chess to while away the long hours of winter darkness. All these things Jan loved, but Brus liked better the other part of their training; handling of weapons, hawking, managing the dogs and horses.

The twin boys, though scarcely men, at thirteen were able to do almost a man's work. They could swim like seals, could stay under water for minutes, and could dive from great heights. Even as children they had been under strict discipline. They could outrun all the boys on the holding and could jump almost their own height, forward or backward.

"We know how to rig the ship," said Brus, "and how to stand at the steering board."

"Aye," said Jan excitedly.

"We know, too, how to calk her and make her seaworthy; and how to get her ashore, safe from the tide."

"We can bend an oar, too, if need be," added Brus.

"Aye, we have many skills," agreed Jan, "even the longbow. I'm glad our father taught us, for 'tis said that in Britain they use well the longbow."

"I've heard 'tis so," Brus answered, "but no Englander may outdo *me* with the longbow! Remember you, how, in the contest with Eirik, the Earl's son, I split his arrow with mine own?"

"I have not forgotten that one!" said Jan. "Remember you how *I* sent my arrow into the tree and pinned fast the sleeve of our uncle?"

" 'Twas a good shot, my brother," admitted Brus. "But you do not so well as I with the dirk. You are too gentle for hand-fighting and like not the sight of blood."

"Aye," said Jan ruefully, "swift you are, and terrible. As for me, I have no stomach for it."

"We have slept out in all weathers," said Brus, "and have gone without food for long. We are ready for what may come on sea or land."

The next day Harald came riding back in the late afternoon. He had lost the angry, puzzled frown of the day before and looked at peace. He hailed the boys as he came into the courtyard.

"Come to the supper meal, my sons," he said. "There is much to tell and much to do before the ships can be launched. They must be calked after the long winter on the beach and all repairs made, new paint added and new oars fitted. We go a-Viking." (As if they hadn't known.)

He dismounted and the horse was led away. They went into the hall where the table was laid, and maids were busy bringing food.

A fire burned in the center fire hearth, sending the smoke

15

out through the roof. The family sat in the high seat. The thralls, the stableboys, the herders sat on wall benches with their food on their laps. Over each place hung weapons and cloaks, caps and extra clothing, for here was their sleeping place as well.

Brus and Jan devoured their meal of smoked meat and hard bread, eager to hear what their father had to say, but he was hungry and took his time over food and ale. At last he was finished and began to speak.

"You, my men, and your womenfolk are ready to follow us to the land of the Englar. That I know, as I know you owe me allegiance, and I have talked with you and know your willingness.

"There shall be three ships; mine, *Raven of the Wind,* and those two of my father's I long have used, which now are mine.

"Into the first ship with me go the warriors, and my sons, Brus and Jan, to defend the others in case of attack. Into the second ship, the *Hawk,* with Ragnhild, your mistress, goes Catriona, once nurse to my sons, and who came from the Western Isles; she can act as interpreter, if need be. The women and the children of your families also go in the second ship with the house carls, for a crew to guide her and to man the oars if wind should fail. Into the third ship, the *Sea Wolf,* with her crew, go the horses, two milch cows, a crate of geese, and the hounds.

"Most of the cattle and herds I have left with Agnar, my foster brother. Now," Harald went on, "leave us. There are matters of family to discuss." The servants went out, leaving the family.

Then Harald told how he and Agnar had sat over the bargaining table. In exchange for the cattle and his holding of

16

land and houses, he had received certain moneys for outfitting the voyage, and title to the *Hawk* and the *Sea Wolf*, both of which had seen long service. Besides these things Agnar had given him an ancient brooch, long a talisman of the family. It had been a part of the booty brought from the Franks two centuries before. The jewel was a shoulder pin for holding the cloak in place. It was round in shape, curiously wrought with intertwining symbols engraved on silver gilt, and set with garnet and sapphire, with topaz and emerald.

It was thought that the brooch had mystic power to keep its wearer from evil and from head wounds. But should he happen to hear a wolf howl under an ash tree, the magic power would be lost. It became like any breast pin set with gems, of value for itself alone.

When Agnar had offered the jewel as part payment for the cattle, Harald had protested. He knew the jewel was a family treasure partly because of its antiquity.

"Tell me truly, Agnar, will fortune fly from you if you part with it? And if it pass into my hands, will it lose its power for good, and instead, be an evil token? I am a foster son. You are eldest and true son. Always the eldest has kept it. Give me now some lesser token. I hold no anger because you have taken what is yours, though long have I held the grazing place in the high field, and long has the forest been mine for the using."

"No, no," Agnar had said, "Take you this. I give it freely. It is a fair thing you leave me, the holding of land above the fiord, the houses, the cattle and sheep. Besides, I have still a powerful talisman, the sword of Ohtor, and other things of value to pass on to my children; things taken as booty when I also went a-Viking. Take you this jewel as a token of remembrance from your kinsmen who keep the land of our fathers."

18

Agnar then had fastened the brooch to Harald's cloak and sealed the bargain with a handclasp, bidding him farewell.

"There are fine cattle in that herd," said Harald with a sigh, "but we shall find good beasts in Britain. In the Western Isles, there are native cattle, long-horned and shaggy. They look out through bushy hair that hangs over their eyes. There are native sheep as well. They have long yellowish faces like the face of Einar's old wife, and thick wool that makes good cloth. With my own eyes I have seen it."

"Go we then to the Western Isles?" asked Jan.

"No," said Harald, "we go to the near shores of Britain, where already the Danes have a foothold. 'Tis but a short three or four days' voyage, if the sea gods be kind. The lands are good for growing and there is room for settling. Heming the Dane showed us much booty and tribute won from that coast, when last we met in Jutland. There is a place called 'Skald Thorp' in Northumbria where the Danes hold sway, and good farm land is. All doors should be searched to know where foes sit, for Saxons may have taken back the land. One must be wary, but not too wary, for oft where one looks for foes, one finds friends.

"Even among our men there are those who may prove false. One who is uncertain in temper, a troublemaker, is Birger Harelip; yet he fears naught, and he knows the path of the sea. He has a strong arm with the sword and a sure hand at the helm. But Birger Harelip I must watch, lest he go berserk. For the words that a man says to another he has often to pay penalty.

"Then, Thurgil, though a good man, is old; he can no longer wield a broadsword or carry a shield. But he still is wise in the ways of the sea, and sometimes it is good what old men say. Skilled words come often out of a shriveled skin."

"Will there be battle" asked Brus hopefully.

"Aye, will there?" echoed Jan, not so hopefully. Brus was ever eager for battle and for killing. If they hunted the deer, Brus was always first to let the arrow fly. If they snared small beasts, or birds, Brus shouted with joy at their capture. Jan thought of the mothers bereft of their young, and could not look into the eyes of the slain ones.

"Battle there may be, truly, but no man goes forth till he has proven himself," Harald answered.

"One thing I must tell you," he counseled. "Oft have you made fools of your mother and of me, with one of you taking the place of the other because you are like as two herring drawn from the fiord. It can be an advantage to you. Always, when in strange place or circumstance, let you keep apart. If foes be near and one be captured, one may still be free and able to loose the other, so not all be lost. If it chanced that one be captured, the other might at times be able to take his place and do the thing he does best, since you have differing skills, thus securing good will from his captor or finding ways of escape. Think on this."

Some weeks later, when it was near summer though still un-settled weather, the ships had been rolled on logs, slipped into the water, and anchored. There they were fitted with steering gear, with long oars, and oarlocks. The stem smith had fitted a new dragon head to the *Raven*. There was new bright paint on all three ships and gold leaf glittered from the dragon heads and tails at prow and stern. New sails of two-fold, well-woven cloth were hung from the mast and at the top were streamers of silk in Harald's colors, the gold of his hair, which was a halo about his head, and the red of his beard which fanned out over his barrel-like chest.

Into the first ship with the fighting men went long swords, spears, and shields, yew bows and arrows, chain mail, and short swords. All were stored in the high seat-chest in the prow. The shields were hung outside along the gunwale. Casks of ale and water were set about the mast. Tents and a supply of food were stored with the leather sleeping bags in the sleeping place.

Into the second ship went the clothing, the stores of grain and the querns for grinding, smoked meats, cheeses, pickled herring, dried fruits, and hard bread. In the stern, where the women slept, went the carved high seat, the beds Ragnhild had brought with her marriage dowry, and linens woven from the flax grown on the holding.

Aboard the third ship went hay and fodder for the animals, a food supply for the crew, and last of all the horses and the two cows, the two hounds, and the geese.

When all was ready, the whole company of men, women, and children came trooping down to go aboard, each laden with some forgotten thing; some treasure too dear to be left. Friends and relations followed, shouting farewell messages, waving kerchiefs, and wiping away tears. Brus and Jan were beside their father in the *Raven* high in the prow, happy to be venturing forth, thinking only of new lands to be seen and conquered, perhaps battles to be fought and won, and the strange people of Britain to be met and known, for there they would live henceforth.

Ragnhild, the mother, stood with the women at the side of the *Hawk* and looked with longing eyes at the rocky steeps of home; the blue of the fiord, the green of spruce. She twisted round and round the armlet of silver that had been her mother's and her grandmother's. She thought of the sons she had borne here; of Hardi and Bran, who had gone forth and never returned, then of Brus and Jan, standing so tall and strong beside their father.

"Farewell," she said aloud. "Farewell, my land, my kinfolk. Farewell."

The three ships were a brave sight as they set forth out of the harbor. The wind was fair and early-morning clear and rosy.

"Red dawn means rough sea," said Harald as they came out into open water. And so it was.

In the night the sky clouded over, strong winds rose to a gale, and the waves were very great. The ship in the lead went swiftly, for it was strong and slender and built for heavy seas. The ships following, though well built, were not so fast, for they were designed to hold gear and animals for merchant shipping; and one, the third ship, was very old.

The second day, when they were far out to sea, the waves were as mountains, the sea began to move fearfully as if monsters had been beneath. The air filled with snow, so nought could be seen from the *Raven* of the ships following except now and then a glimpse of blue and gold prow or a flicker of sail.

"We shall make for the Orkneys," shouted Harald to Snorri at the steering board. *"Furl sail!"* he bellowed to the crewmen. *"Man the oars and cast anchor!* We shall wait for the others to come up."

They held the ship as best they could, but the sea raced by the gunwale as if the sail had been full set. Search as they might, they could find no sign of the *Hawk* or of the *Sea Wolf*.

Toward the second night Harald's ship came near the islands off Scotland. The snow ceased falling and they were able to go into the harbor, where they stayed the night. Harald himself kept watch with one of the men, in case of enemies and in hope the other ships might come in sight, but even morning brought no sign of them. The storm seemed over and all was calm, so they made for open sea again, spread sail, and set out to find the two lost ships.

"Can our mother be taken by the sea god," asked Jan of his father fearfully, "and all our household made to serve him?"

"Our father will find them," boasted Brus, "never fear."

"It may be Ragnhild, thy mother, is death-fated," Harald said, "and will spread linen for her bed in Neptune's chamber. But if the witch storm sleeps, we may yet find the *Hawk* and *Sea Wolf*, and go again to our course."

There was a fair wind for a while. Then it grew stronger and changed direction, and when they had passed the lee of the islands, waves came again over the ship's side in a pounding torrent. Rain mixed with snow came down in a blinding curtain, as it sometimes did in late spring. Some of the men bailed furiously, while others, with difficulty, furled sail. The helmsman could not hold the ship to any course but must needs go where the winds willed.

Harald stood high in the prow, searching the horizon with his keen eyes; Brus and Jan with him, one at either side. Sea water washed over them again and again, and the freezing wind off the North Sea blued their lips and set teeth chattering. Still they stood watching.

Jan saw how Harald fingered the jeweled clasp of his wet cloak. He wondered if its magic would bring forth the missing ones. He saw his father's lips move as he said over and over the ship's name: "*Raven of the Wind—Raven of the Wind*." How many times his father had gone forth in the *Raven* and come back safely. He thought of the *Hawk*, the ship of the women, how it was wide and deep, its timbers sturdy. Then he thought of the third ship, the *Sea Wolf*, with its cargo of animals, and the men who guided her, with Gunnar standing at the helm. "Let the sea gods be kind," he prayed hopefully.

"Of the third ship, I have little hope," shouted Harald, seeing terror in the boys' eyes. "She was old, and scarce seaworthy, having carried many a cargo to Trondhjeim and Jutland. Yet we can pray the gods carry the ships safely over the waves and lift them into some safe harbor. Brus, hold fast the helm with Snorri! Jan, help tie that loosened sheet rope."

For three days the *Raven* was tossed about, half the men at the oars, half of them bailing out the sea, having no rest day or night. They took food when Brus or Jan crept on hands and knees to the store place under the deck to get hard bread and salt meat.

"There's little time for food with death so near," said Harald. "Sing of the heroes!" he cried. "Sing! 'Twill hearten us all, and 'twill show the sea witch that we fear not to die!"

So the men sang, though sword belts hung loose from hunger, arms grew slack from pulling at oars, and eyelids smarted from sea water.

On the fourth day the winds died. It was possible to survey what damage the ship had suffered. Much gear had been lost, shields from the gunwale, some of the oars, and rope from the rigging. The bright paint was faded, and the tip of the mast gone with its gay streamers.

But all men were alive on the *Raven,* though none knew where he stood, whether in the North Sea or in other waters.

"Even I, Harald, sea warrior that I am, know not where the ship stands, whether toward the east coast of Britain, Iceland, or toward the Western Isles.

" 'Tis not good to be lost, but one who travels widely must meet good and evil. From the look of the sea, and the way of the wind, I would say we are set toward the Western Isles. A sight of land would soon tell, for if we are there, as I think, land would be to larboard, or if we chanced to be among the isles, land would be on both sides."

But mist surrounded them and lay low on the water, so nothing could be seen. It seemed as if it were lifting for a moment, then it came down as thick as before.

Brus went aloft, hoping to see above the fog, but when he reached the top of the broken mast, he could see no more than below. The sea began to heave again in great rolls. The wind came up astern, and the ship rushed forward carried by a great wave bobbing about like the tops he and Jan used to spin.

Brus had much ado to hold fast. Rain followed the wind, lashing at him, making the mast slippery. Loosened sail cord whipped about him, as if punishing him for work left undone.

All was confusion below. Brus saw two of the men tossed into the sea, and though they were strong swimmers, the current was so great they could not rise above it and were lost to sight.

Once, when the mast swayed out over the sea, Brus thought he, too, could no longer hold on and would be lost. Then, for an instant, the mast righted itself, he slipped below the yardarm, and swiftly down, losing his hold before he struck deck and landing somewhat bruised but, for the moment, safe.

Jan, too, had thought his brother lost when the ship swayed so wildly and had made his way to the rowing bench before the mast, where he could reach Brus as he fell. Holding fast to the brace of the bench, he pulled Brus toward him and together they crept beneath the rowing seat till the ship should cease its flinging about.

Another sudden gust lifted the fog, as if a giant hand had

carried it aloft, and by the same magic brought a rocky coast out of the sea, for the rocks rose up on every hand, seeming to race toward the ship as if the land moved instead of the ship.

Brus and Jan could not see the new danger from where they were sheltered, but Harald, who still hugged the prow, could see well in the clearing light.

He saw disaster. The coast was very near, and Harald knew that where rocks line a shore they also hide beneath water. With a tearing, crushing sound, the hull of the ship was pierced and water rushed through.

"All hands astern!" Harald roared. *"Leave the shi-i-ip!"*

Brus and Jan looked at each other, each vowing in silence to cling together to the end. They heard their father's voice, mourning the calamity he foresaw.

"We perish!" he groaned. "Our songs of merriment are sung. The sea gods laugh at us."

All men left whatever their clinging hands held, oar, mast, or rigging.

They crept toward the stern as best they could, from bench to bench, from mast to gunwale. A tremendous wave came over, washing away everything not fastened down, throwing men to the deck, carrying away part of the bow, and flinging four into the sea, one of them Snorri the helmsman.

The others got to their feet and leaped after him, one by one; each laughed as he went overboard at the grim game they played, laughed and shouted in farewell.

Helgi first:

"We, the warriors, lose this battle to the sea witch!" he cried.

Then Thorfinn:

"Nevermore shall oar locks weary this arm!" he shouted, and leaped into the sea.

26

Then Bjorn:

"Tonight, I feast with the gods!" He went down.

However they went, whatever they spoke in leaving, every man of them laughed in face of death.

"We, too, are men, my brother," said Brus as they stood in turn and followed the others.

When all had gone, Harald stood for an instant, free of the prow, feet wide apart, arms uplifted.

"SEA WITCH! DO YOUR WORST!" he shouted.

The rocks raced toward him as he plunged into the tumbling water and swam free just as the ship seemed to burst into the pieces of which it had been built. The timbers leaped into the air, then fell back into the sea among the struggling warriors.

Some of the men were cast upon the rocks.

Some managed to reach quieter water and walk ashore.

Some were thrown aside in the surf and cast upon the shingle. Some were drowned.

Brus and Jan kept together and floated ashore on a fragment of mast.

Harald, though carried down shore and tossed about by the waves, was finally able to get himself beyond their reach. He lay quiet to recover breath, as did all who were saved, then joined the others to find his sons safe and unhurt.

"Death was likelier than life, this voyage," he said, embracing them. "Now, let us be thankful to the gods some of our company have been spared and that I still have two sons left me.

"Which warriors lost the battle?" Harald took stock of the men and counted sixteen missing from the thirty who had begun the voyage.

"Sixteen Vikings are lost to us," he said mournfully, naming them one by one, "Sigmund, Helgi, Bjorn, Thorfinn, Eyvar, Snorri"—and on——to the very end.

"There will be sorrowing," he said, "but this we must take as it is. Once, every man must die, and 'tis said, Neptune gives a soft bed and quiet sleep."

Fourteen men were left besides Harald Redbeard and his sons, Brus and Jan.

2   Because it was into summer, darkness was long in coming. Those who had been saved thought it safe to build a fire in the shelter of rock, to dry clothing and cook salt meat that had washed ashore. Of bread there was none. Of clothing, only that which they wore. Of firewood there was plenty; broken boards, splintered mast, and oars washed ashore

with every wave. Flint and tinder were dry in Harald's box of carved walrus tusk. Shavings, cut with a belt knife, soon set the fire alight. All other weapons were at the bottom of the sea.

There was no water, no ale, for the casks had been cracked by the falling mast. Jan, searching along the shore, discovered a waterfall, and a climb up the rocky steep led to the burn, or stream, which fed it.

He carried water in Harald's helmet and gave him first to drink. He was much wearied and beaten by the waves. Jan went a second time for water. He filled the helmet, and when he raised himself from the edge of the burn, a man stood over him. A man who frowned down from a great height, his arms folded over a deep chest. At his side hung a great sword, at his belt, a dirk. Into his stocking a knife was thrust.

His draw-kirtle hung only to his knees, which were bare, for the thick wool stocking started below them. The man spoke. "Who art thou?" he demanded. "Who are thy friends?"

Jan straightened, giving him stare for stare, placing his hand on his belt knife, saying nought. The words he heard were somewhat strange in the manner of speaking. "Yet," thought Jan, "They are like the words our nurse Catriona taught us. But, of course, she was captured in a raid on the Western Isles."

Jan's scalp prickled, his nostrils quivered. Was this, then, his first enemy?

"Take me to thy friends," he was commanded.

Then, without warning, such a shriek rent the air that Jan's hair rose from his scalp.

"*A-gael! A-gael!*" came the cry from the stranger's throat as he beckoned with his large hand.

In an instant, out of the earth, it seemed, sprang warriors, about thirty in number, armed, like their chief, with sword, dirk, and stocking knife.

"This young cock trespasses on our land," said the chief. "Watch him." They closed around Jan. "Take us to the camp," he directed shortly.

The camp was alerted and afoot long before the two companies sighted each other, for the clan cry carried far. Brus had time to heed his father's warning and lay hidden behind a rock in the gorse which grew wherever a bit of soil gave it root.

"Be wary," cautioned Harald, "as I bade you. Jan has perhaps been taken. It may be your likeness to him will be of service now. Keep far from him whether ill or good betides. For if a stranger speaks loudly, he may be friend, or if he speaks softly, he may be foe. Go warily, and keep apart from your brother."

Each man clasped his belt knife, ready to fight for his life, but hoping for peace.

Harald put on his cloak, still wet, and fastened the jewel on his shoulder. Brus saw it gleam in the sunlight. Let it prove a powerful talisman! Let the gods be kind!

The clansmen could be heard clattering over the stone scree to the shore.

"Hail! Thou of the ruddy beard!" called the chief, who led the others. "What *do* you here in Bègan's land?"

The tall Scot faced the red-bearded Harald, and his words came out in great round burrs. The words were difficult for Harald to understand, even though he had many times heard the twins chattering with Catriona.

"If we trespass," Harald said, " 'tis not by our choosing. Here were we cast ashore, spewed up from the sea god's mouth. We came on peaceful mission, meaning to settle and to stay on

Britain's east coat, where we have kinsmen among the Danes."

"Came you in one ship, then, alone?"

"Aye," said Harald, "alone. Two of our ships we lost off the Orkneys, and search as we might, we could not find them. The storm drove us here and split our ship asunder."

"I am Bègan Mòr," said the giant, "Thane of Skye, the Winged Isle, and of lands beyond the strait. By conquest this is *my* domain. You, I perceive, are a chieftain also. Let us talk further of this matter. Tonight, we feast on yon table mountain where my castle is, to celebrate the betrothal of my daughter, Nineag, to the Laird of Lorne. Come you with your warriors." He gestured largely in the direction of a flat-topped high rock not far distant and, putting a heavy hand on Jan's shoulder, said, "This young knave we shall take with us. I count fourteen of your men. Let every man be there!" Without further words he made a sign of farewell, and, keeping Jan in the midst of the group, went off.

"It may be he thinks fair as he speaks," said Harald. "We are few and not in full strength after our sea beating, else I would strike him aside as I would crush a fly, and claim my son. He means we shall attend his banquet whether we will or no."

He called Brus to come out of hiding and charged him to fit himself with courage and with whatever food and weapon they could find. "This night," he said, "is the time to take advantage of the likeness to your brother. Use it well. Stay apart from us and from Jan and thus perhaps help to save him and us. If ye be seen, it may be thought you are your brother.

"Mind thy temper, Birger Harelip. 'Twill need but a spark to light the fire of trouble. Lift seldom the drinking horn and keep from evil ale-talk. What have we now to leave with Brus? What store of food?"

32

Ola put salt meat into a pouch for Brus.

Sven took off his cloak and fastened it round him.

Fergus gave him his wooden spoon, and Sigurd, a small, carved token of amber. It was in the shape of Thor's hammer, smooth to the touch and worn with handling.

" 'Tis a comforting thing to hold," said Sigurd. "When one has anxious thoughts, and must wait in patience, 'tis good to remember Thor's strength," he said.

Brus knew Sigurd was thinking of how long the hours would be for himself while the others were at the feast and would know how things were going.

Brus said little, but recalled the ways he and Jan used to

communicate with one another secretly. They used bird calls, the call of the loon, the cry of the bittern, the screech of the sea mew, repeated a certain way. Sometimes they used a wolf howl with a slight sound following to distinguish it; the yowl of a cat or the grunt of a wild pig. It depended upon where they happened to be when the need came. Here, he thought, the cry of the sea mew would be lost, for circling gulls screamed continually. He would wait and see. Perhaps Jan would give him a signal.

As the men of the island went away into the distance, a wild kind of music could be heard. It sounded almost human, a voice wailing, mournful, yet exciting. Brus's scalp tingled at the hearing of it.

Harald saw the wondering look in Brus's eyes.

" 'Tis the pibroch of the bagpipe," he said, "beloved of the people of this country. There will be more of it at the feast we attend. Now, let us look to our belt knives and count what protection is left us. Let every man at the feast be wary. 'Tis like to be a feast for carrion birds at the ending. Yet, it may be this chieftain means friendship, and we shall walk away in safety."

Each man fared forth as brave as might be in what garments were left, girded with belt knife, which always accompanied him. They left the camp as well arranged for shelter as they were able, with the driftwood and the few objects that had floated ashore.

"Sleep here we may *not*," said Harald as they left the camp. "Ere this midsummer night turns to dawn, it may be we shall sleep in heather, purpled before its blossoming time with our lifeblood. Come! Let us to it!"

They left the stony beach and climbed to the ridge. Before

reaching the top Harald once more cautioned Brus about keeping himself hidden and apart.

"Every shadow may hold danger, every bush an enemy's sword," said Harald. "Move slowly."

"Now," promised Brus to himself, as he went warily from one clump of gorse to another, from one rocky heap to the next, "our father shall see that we are men. Jan will prove himself worthy of the chieftain's company, and I keep so careful a watch that nothing shall escape me."

The sky still held a golden sun when the company reached the flat-topped mount, above which rose a battlement and the thatched roof of the "dun," or castle, and the top of the keep. The stronghold was crude, not much like the handsome, well-built ones Brus had known at home in Norway. The great rock on which the castle stood rose straight up from the sea loch and had but a narrow approach at one side, which, Brus could see, would be covered with water at high tide. The only entrance was by a flight of stone steps carved out of the rock leading to a doorway. Brus had followed as closely as he dared, keeping hidden till the whole company, led by his father, had arrived at the top of the deep passage that pierced the rock and opened into the broad courtyard. Flattening himself in a curve of the passage, Brus waited till the guard of the clansmen had counted all strangers, knowing that soon the tide would cover all approach. Brus scarcely breathed, he kept so still. He felt the smooth amber token in his hand and hoped it, too, would prove a good talisman. The guard, reassured, left the head of the stair and went to other duties.

Brus crept carefully upward, through the water gate, up and up, till he could distinguish the voices of the guards and the servants at the cooking place. He kept his head below the level of the courtyard till he was sure he would not be seen.

Meantime Jan had fared well with his captors. The chief had questioned him, but Jan was brief in answering, though courteous. He had found a great gathering of people on the mount and tremendous preparations for the feast. Huge fires blazed, over which whole oxen were roasting; caldrons of steaming brew hung from iron supports. Casks and baskets, hampers and buckets stood about where the cooking place was. The seats of the chief and other nobles and their ladies stood behind a stone slab resting upon rocks that were rooted in the mount. It was set with drinking horns, wooden bowls and trenchers.

One of the ladies, Jan thought, was like his mother, though her dress was different. A wave of homesickness swept through him. What had become of his mother? Was she really death-fated? Or could it be that the gods had been kind and set her ashore in some safe place. But where?

The voice of the chieftain brought him back.

"Young knave! Sit you here! Here—where we can watch whether ye be friend or foe! Fellow clansmen," he went on, addressing the gathering, "we have other guests who have come unbidden to our isle. Here we have one of their warriors!" A derisive sweep of his great hand gestured toward Jan. "Behold his fierce look! See the array of weapons he carries to conquer Bègan Mòr!" He roared forth a hearty laugh that was caught up by those near, and grew and grew till it swept through the whole company. Even the womenfolk tittered, and the girl Nineag, standing beside the chieftain, looked at Jan and giggled.

Jan didn't like being laughed at, least of all by strangers. For once he longed to bring forth his belt knife—to swing about with it—to see blood flow. His blue eyes blazed back at the girl

36

angrily, but he could not help seeing she was fair. The long yellow braids which hung over her shoulders were twined with ribbon and with flowers. Her dress was silken like that of Norway's queen, whom Jan had seen at the district gathering last year. Jan wished she had not laughed.

As the laughter died, a turning of heads told Jan that Harald and his men had arrived. He stood more straight and prideful, holding fast to all his teaching, and wondering where Brus might be.

Jan wished Brus had been there to see the fair Nineag, with her silken gown and flower-decked hair, though Brus would think him soft for looking at a woman, be she ever so fair.

Bègan Mòr directed the seating of Harald's men, putting Harald next himself, and, at lower tables, each one of Harald's men between two of his own. Jan was near the high seats where sat the nobles and their ladies. There was a bearded old man who, Jan thought, might be like the scalds of Norway. Near him was a younger man, dressed in sober gown and cowl, whose head was shaven in a circlet of hair. Beads hung from his belt, ending in a wooden cross. He said he was a monk from Ireland, come to bring the gospel of Christ to the Winged Isle and to Scotland.

Jan's eyes rested on the vast quantities of food that were set before them; joints of beef, bowls of oaten porridge mixed with herbs, great round loaves of oaten bread. 'Twas fair mouth-watering, when days of storm had so emptied the belly. The servers brought ewers of ale to fill the huge drinking horns, and the wooden mugs of lesser folk. They were filled, not once, but many times, so that some were merry and there was much laughter.

But Brus *had* seen.

He had seen it all, even Nineag the Fair. As the sun sank low
and the feasting began to be noisy, Brus crept to the very top
of the water stair, putting his cloak over his head to cover his
bright hair from the glint of the firelight. He could see the
whole company beyond the moving figures of the servants
across the open space around which the tables were set. For
when daylight faded and twilight rested on the land, torches
were lit and thrust into cracks in the rock, throwing over the
feast a ruddy, eerie light. Voices seemed to ring on the stone
of wall and paving, so Brus could hear as well as see. He could
see Jan and Jan's neighbor, the monk, and all of Harald's men.

Bègan Mòr stood to announce the betrothal.

"Nobles, friends," he began, his great voice booming forth,
"we are gathered here this eve to celebrate the betrothal of our
daughter, Nineag, to Gavin Dhu of Lorne." He bade the young
people to rise, and joined their hands, then went on speaking.

"When the snows of winter come and we have the Christ
Mass, then shall the wedding be, and two great houses joined
and great stretch of lands. Let no man think to find place here!"
He turned to Harald, as if in warning. "Else, he shall find
instead a two-edged sword!"

A shout went up. Drinking horns were raised, swords lifted
to pledge allegiance. The pipers tuned up, marching around
and around and in and out among the guests, their wild music
setting Brus aquiver to join in the revel. The smell of food
was a torture to his empty middle, so he took the salt meat from
his purse to chew on, which only made him the more thirsty.
The sight of the ale servers passing with ewers to fill mugs and
drinking horns was a continual torment. He took out the amber
token to smooth in his hands and tried to remember the discipline of days on the mountains of Norway without food. He

could hear his father's voice saying, "To be a Viking, one must be ready, ready for what the gods send of good or evil."

Brus saw the white-bearded old man rise, the soothsayer. He listened to hear his tale; the story of the deeds of the warriors of old, as the scald had used to do at the gatherings in his homeland, half sung, half intoned. He told it from the beginning of time, as much as was known, the generations of kings and thanes who had ruled that part of the Western Isles and the land of the Scots; how once the land had belonged to ancient Celtic tribes called Picts, because of their habit of tattooing their skins. They had lived in the Highlands in caves and huts, and built towers of refuge called "brochs." They had fought the Gaelic tribes, called Scots, that had come from North Ireland in the sixth century, but, after hundreds of years of fighting, had finally joined with them against invading Danes and Norsemen.

("Invaders!" thought Brus. " 'Tis *invaders* they think us to be!")

The soothsayer went on—telling how at times the Picts and Scots still fought one tribe against the other, and how wandering Pictish tribes sometimes raided villages and beset travelers. Now this castle and the Winged Isle, on which it stood, belonged to Bègan Mòr, who claimed it by conquest, and who now gave vassalage to Malcolm II, King of the Scots. He claimed, as well, the land across the strait, as far as Loch Shiel. Beyond was the country of Cam-Ron, sheriff and thane of the Glen.

"There," said the soothsayer, "to Cam-Ron of the Glen, sheriff, must tribute be paid or battle fought, or all the journey come to naught. . . ." Brus listened to every word, though the tale was long and unfamiliar, remembering how his father had

40

told him to keep ears and eyes open, for it might be useful to know who claimed the lands hereabout, whether by conquest or inheritance.

The soothsayer went on.

"Gavin Dhu, the Laird of Lorne, with lip beard black, his chin all shorn, hath this day to Nineag the Fair, the gentle maid with flower-decked hair, been handfast promised this summer's eve and in winter's cold shall they take their leave, and two clans the now unite, Gavin the Black and Nineag the White. He keepeth a fortress five days hence, a fortress strong in their defense. One day's travel on this isle to yon narrow strait, where in low tide, the horses' gait across the water then may go. Through mountain pass and lochs across, through wood and glen, o'er burn and brae, till to Dundugal they come at last. So will the wedding at Christ Mass bring great strongholds together for Scotland's king!" He sat down among clapping hands and laughter and shouts of "Scotland! Scotland!"

Before the piping began again, the monk rose and begged leave to tell his story.

He told of a holy man, St. Columba, who had left Ireland centuries before to bring the gospel of Christ to the savage men of early Scotland, then called Skotia. He had lived with other holy men dedicated to the service of their Lord on Iona, a small isle to the south. There, kings were taken to be buried when their life on earth was finished. To the Holy Isle they were carried in boats from a resting place in that same country of Lorne, to which pilgrims in solemn procession bore them. Then the monk told of the Christ, the Son of God, who drew all men unto Him because He had died for all men. Because of His lowly birth in a manger, His life of toil in a carpenter's shop, He was kindred with lowly men. Because of His nobility,

41

His kinship with God, He understood the thoughts of even the most learned men. When those who understood Him not persecuted Him and nailed Him to a cross, He forgave them for their ignorance and rose again from the dead that all men might know His way of life and follow it.

Brus listened to the very end. "It is the saga of a noble man," he thought, "but what of the old gods? Why speaks he not of them? Of Odin and Thor and Freya?" He remembered how Harald, their father, had told of Olaf Tryggvessön, who had been King, and how he had forced some of his subjects to accept the Christian religion or suffer death. Harald had not been one of them. He had said that he and his house would keep to the old ways of Odin and Thor, of Loki, the god of mischief, and the sea god, who was sometimes kind, but was often fierce. "The sea god!" he thought. "Never was the sea god less kind than on this voyage. Never struck Thor's hammer so hard as now!"

Like Jan, he wondered where the other ships could be. Did their mother sleep beneath the tossing waves? Did she sleep? Or, did she go about as womenfolk do, caring for the sea god's warriors, mending their clothes, weaving their mantles and long hosen? What had become of her and all their household? These thoughts went swiftly through Brus's head in the pause at the ending of the monk's tale. Then the monk held up the wooden cross for all to see.

"By this sign shall ye conquer!" he cried. "The love of God keep your hearts and minds!"

And every man of Bègan Mòr, the nobles and their ladies, made the sign, touching forehead and breast, with head bowed and solemn look. Brus saw Bègan Mòr stand, and beside him Harald, his father, stood also. They clasped hands and drank

42

together. Perhaps it betokened friendship between them. Brus looked to the men, his father's warriors sitting among Bègan Mòr's men. They seemed friendly enough, though they had forgotten Harald's warning, for as oft as the wooden mugs were filled with ale, they were emptied and filled again.

Bègan Mòr gestured toward Jan, who rose at his bidding.

"Come now, thou youthling!" cried the chief. "Let us hear how ye fared on yon North Sea! Sing us a saga for thy supper!"

Then Jan sang. Brus listened carefully, for by what Jan said in the ballad, and the way he said it, Brus might discover what signal he should use to let Jan know he heard him. Jan sang of the voyage, the setting forth, the storm, the loss of the two ships, the wreck of the *Raven,* and of those left. The song went:

> *Harald and his men set out*
> *In ships three went a-Viking.*
> *The ships were brave with painted sail,*
> *And carved prows to their liking.*

> *Harald in the* Raven *went*
> *First of the three defending.*
> *Storm drove him fast, on rock at last,*
> *Ship and venture ending.*

> *Oh, sing of the sea king,*
> *Sing of the storm,*
> *Sing of the wives*
> *That are all forlorn.*

> *Two ships were lost in waters cold*
> *Mid storm and wind a-blowing.*
> *The sea witch hid them from our sight,*
> *Though men grew weary rowing.*

Oh, sing of the sea king,
Sing of the storm,
Sing of the wives
That are all forlorn.

The Sea Wolf *had good men aboard,*
Horses and cattle keeping,
With Lars and Vigi standing watch
While cattle were a-sleeping.

The Hawk *was broad and strong and deep*
At her prow stood Thurgil the Knowing,
Guarding the mother and womenfolk
While a wild sea was a-flowing.

Oh, sing of the sea king,
Sing of the storm,
Sing of the sons
That are all forlorn.

Oh, men were drowned in the fathomless deep
And where are the wives forlorn?
In the sea god's palace with mermaids sleep
Like the dove, we are left to m-o-u-r-n!

Oh, sing of the sea king,
Sing of the storm,
Sing of the sons
That are left to m-o-u-r-n!

As Jan sang again the word "mourn," he drew it out, emphasizing it, and letting his voice rise, as if trying to make Brus hear, wherever he might be. Brus took this to be a signal to declare himself and let Jan know where he was. He dared not

44

make a sound where he stood, so quickly he flew down the water stair and from outside the wall, in the pause and hand clapping that followed the singing of the ballad, he made the mournful sound of the wood dove, repeating it three times, then changing it slightly in tone, and making the sound twice more: "ooOooo! ooOooo! ooOooo!—oo! oo!" That had been their signal at home in Norway when they had been separated, and each must stay for the moment where he was. Now it told Jan that Brus was near. When he heard laughter and hand clapping begin again, Brus once more crept up the water stair, where he could see over the parapet. How he wished one of the servants would chance to drop a joint of beef on his way back to the cooking place, or even a chunk of bread.

When he reached the top of the stair, there was so much noise and laughter he could not hear what went forward at the high seat, though he could see Bègan Mòr lifting his great gold-tipped drinking horn. Now that the revel was becoming boisterous, the ladies and their women rose and left the feast to the menfolk. It was time for men's games and feats of strength; for wrestling, spear throwing; for dirk and sword-play.

When Jan had heard the story of the Christ told by the Irish monk, and how He had given His Life for all men on a cross, he thought it a wondrous tale.

But did no one love this Christ, then, not to avenge Him?

Had He no brothers to slay those who had killed Him?

Jan looked about the company to see how they took this

strange story. All men listened with grave faces, cruelty gone out of them for the moment.

The women gazed with tear-dimmed eyes at the gentle monk as he held up the cross. The lady Nineag wept sorest of all, for she was very young.

When Jan had sung the ballad and stopped to listen for an answering call, the cry of the wood dove had come to him in that pause before voices were raised again. The same sound he and Brus had often used. He let his ears unstretch. He knew that Brus was not far off. There seemed no way for him to reply, but it was comforting to know Brus was there, free of this uncertain company, and to know he had heard Jan's singing of the ballad. He glanced toward his father to see if he too had recognized the signal, but Harald, if he had heard, wisely gave no sign.

When the women had withdrawn, the games began, the men-at-arms testing their strength at weight lifting, wrestling, fighting with broadswords, shooting at a target with bow and arrow. The chieftain rose and called upon Jan to try his skill with the longbow against the master of Lorne.

"We shall see," he said, "how useful this stripling might be to our daughter's betrothed. We shall give him, if he be worthy, as a present of our grace, a present from Bègan Mòr of the Winged Isle. Let bow and arrows be given him. He hath none of his own." He spoke sneeringly, having dropped the pretense of friendly host.

Jan tried not to look at his father. His face reddened, and his nostrils flared with anger, though he said nought. He was furnished with bow and arrows, the bow of yew as tall as himself, the bowstring of gut very strong. But his arms were strong too from swimming the fiord, from rowing, and from wrestling.

46

This one thing he remembered. Never must one show more skill than his superior in rank. It was not seemly. Now he must watch and do less well than his opponent.

"But," he thought, "perhaps I could not excel him in this, even though I wished, for it is known how skillful are the Britons with the longbow."

Each took his turn, the laird going first, as being of higher rank and guest of honor. He shot straight and true, and very near the center of the target. Then Jan fixed his arrow and aimed, thinking only to come near the mark of the first arrow, but the second arrow split the first one, even as Brus's arrow had split the arrow of the Earl's son last year. Both Bègan Mòr and Gavin Dhu looked annoyed.

"A lucky happening only," said Jan hastily. "I could not do it again." He handed over the bow. But the laird (for that is the way the chief said "lord") insisted they try once more.

"Aye," agreed the chief, "let us see if the cockerel can crow next time. The first time was luck, without doubt, for no one hereabout is keener with the longbow than Gavin of Lorne. Try again, cockerel!"

But a commotion among the men arose.

Shrieks and cries of battle.

A hustling forward of the servants to the high seat with a huge salver. Everyone's attention was toward Bègan Mòr.

"Ha!" exclaimed Bègan. " 'Tis come! Fall to!"

Jan saw with dismay and loathing something which Brus also saw from where he watched; the thing the salver contained.

Jan had not time to recover from the loathsome sight before he saw his father struck down, and he himself was seized and made prisoner. He was hustled into the keep, along a passage, and into a dungeon. There was no need to fasten him with chains, for the wall was very deep, the door heavy and nail-studded.

Before leaving him the guard said grimly, "Beneath this dungeon is another. They who go below come not out, for 'tis bottlenecked and there is no other opening. See! 'Tis where the blackest place is in the floor. But this will serve for an infant." He laughed. "If you wish to live, young cock, stay clear of the black hole. Not that I see what worth you be as hostage." He laughed again, and his laughter echoed and re-echoed against the stone walls that separated Jan from the world.

Jan slipped to the floor and sat with his back to the wall, intending to keep awake, lest he roll toward the opening. For though Harald, their father, had fallen and all seemed lost, Brus still awaited him. Vengeance must be visited upon Bègan Mòr, and they must search for their mother. But the day had been long and fateful. Sleep drew his eyelids down, limbered his spine, and freed him from remembrance and anxious thought.

Brus, from where he watched, saw it all and how it had begun.

He could see Harald's men as they watched the contests, saying little, but by their look, thinking that if *they* had been taking part in the games, they would have won on every count. There had been much drinking of ale, and Birger Harelip was one of those whose cup had been too often filled. He was very noisy. When two of Bègan Mòr's men wrestled in the open space, he began to bait them.

48

"Call you *that* wrestling?" he shouted, showing by his actions what he meant. "Let a *man* show his strength! Birger Harelip can best any man here! Let Birger Harelip contend with any! He shall not last long! He shall go over the wall and into the sea! Wrestling? Bah! Child's play!"

"Thou, Slit-face!" cried the man nearest him, who also had lifted the cup too often. Pointing in derision, he went on, "Try *me,* then!" Both men jumped from their seats.

Birger, enraged by the taunt of "Slit-face" because of his lip, thrust his great hairy hands at the other's throat so that his eyes bulged.

Brus, dismayed, saw the thing happen his father had foreseen. This was the spark to set off trouble. Now were they all in danger.

He became aware of what was being said close by.

"NOW," said the guard. "NOW! 'Tis time! They have broken faith. 'Tis time!"

Brus saw the cooks, the firelight glinting in their eyes, pointing toward something. Something that sent a shiver through him. It was the severed head of a black bull on a platter. The

serving of this gruesome viand was by tradition an evil portent, even in Norway. It meant but one thing.

It meant death to whomever it was served.

The thralls lifted the great salver and hastened through the throng of watchers, housecarls, cooks' assistants, a wrangle of gnawing hounds, then to the place where Harald sat.

The black bull's head was set before him. He drew back in horror, knowing the meaning of it, and started to rise.

Bègan Mòr rose in his place once more.

He raised the clan cry, "A-GAEL! A-GAEL!" And, turning on Harald, smote him over the head with his sword so he fell where he stood. Then every one of Bègan's men who sat one on each side of Harald's, fell upon his neighbor with dirk or sword and slew him, shouting the clan war cry till it echoed and rang through the court in terrifying clamor.

Brus, sick with terror, saw it all, and heard Bègan Mòr's command for the bodies of Harald and his men to be dragged to the wall and thrown over into the loch.

"The tide will carry them away and back to the land from whence they came!" he bellowed.

Brus waited for no more. He flew down the stair and out the water gate. The tide was well up, so he slipped into the water and hid beneath while the gruesome order was carried out; there he stayed till no one looked down from the height above.

Then he pulled himself up the rocky steep to search for his father among the men who had fallen. Jan, too, might be there. But Brus knew that, young as he was, it might be thought he was worth keeping for service, as was the custom with captives.

Though night was at its darkest, this longest day of the year, it was still not very dark. Brus could distinguish faces of those lying on the slope.

50

Some, indeed, had fallen clear of the rocky slope into the sea loch. Some lay stretched where they had fallen, among the heather, purpled, as Harald had said, before its blossoming time.

Where was Harald, their father? Where had he fallen?

Brus searched each face as he found a man; here, face down, was Sigurd, who had given him the amber token, here Sven, here was Hagen, and here was Birger of the split lip, Birger who had unwittingly betrayed them all. And here, last of all, was Harald, his head a mass of blood, down the slope. A tough stem of gorse had kept him from sliding into the loch. Brus, bracing himself with one hand and working with the other, was able to free his father and get him into the water, and swim with him around the base of the mount. It took all his strength to drag him ashore.

He laid his father gently above the tide and stooped to listen whether any breath was in him. A low moan told him his father lived. The talisman had held its power! Brus sighed with relief. Now, to get Harald to a hiding place where he could care for him. Where? Could he leave him long enough to search for a place? There was no other way. He set out, searching among tumbled rocks and trees which surrounded the loch. There were several caves washed out by the sea, but too shallow for hiding. He went around the headland and there found the very spot. Gravel and small stones had washed into an opening in the rock to form the floor of a cavern large enough to hide them, and high enough above the loch for safety. He hurried back. Harald still lay as Brus had left him. He moaned slightly but did not wake to consciousness even when Brus rolled him onto his own cloak, tying the ends about the middle. He took off his father's wide belt and slipped the belt knife in beside his own, then contrived a handhold by which to drag his father across the rocky ledge, then over two intervening points of land and into the cavern.

Before it was accomplished, the tide was full and morning was already breaking over the mist-covered water. There was barely room above the tide to reach the cavern.

Brus unfastened the jewel and removed Harald's cloak, clasping the talisman onto Harald's tunic. He covered him with the cloak—wet though it was. Being of heavy wool, it would keep in the warmth of his body. He dared not make a fire. He threw himself down beside his father and they slept.

3 In the cavern a few hours of sleep brought Harald to consciousness, and strengthening light woke Brus to the need for watchfulness. His first thought was for his father. He raised himself on his elbow to see whether sleep had in any wise healed him. Harald looked at Brus with calm understanding. He spoke.

"Conquerers, we are *not*," he said ruefully. "But we live still, though I know not how it fares with Jan." He looked questioningly at Brus. "Know *you* how it is? Does he live?"

"He lives," answered Brus, "though they took him prisoner."

"And the others? Are any left to us?" Harald went on.

"None," said Brus shortly. He did not trust himself to say more.

"This jeweled amulet I still wear," said Harald. "Perhaps it is not a good omen for me. Yet, I live—though hardly do I live." He paused to gain strength, then spoke again. "When Jan is freed, go in search of your mother. I need not tell you that, but it weighs heavily upon me. What means you will use, I have no head to think on, 'tis so broken." He sighed deeply. "But be ready; ready for what betides, whether good or ill, and be just to all men. . . . I thirst," he said; "there is fever." And again he slept.

Though battle and sudden death were the way of life in that time, and Brus had always known it, this was the first time it had come close to him. He shook his head to clear away the remembrance of those whose bodies he had seen on the steep slope of the mount and rose to get water from the loch to wash away the blood from his father's head. There was nothing he could use to carry water, so he cut a piece of linen from his undergarment, soaked it in the pool left by the tide, which was now low again. Twelve hours from tide to tide! It seemed that in those twelve hours low tide had come to Harald's household as well as to the sea. Would high tide come to them again? Would he and Jan meet once more?

He thought of the jeweled talisman and wondered if it truly held any magic power.

He bathed his father's head and face, going again and again

to the pool for fresh water. He found mussels, which he gathered for food, then set out to find the burn for fresh water, for Harald's skin was very hot. He went cautiously, but once, as he stepped from behind a heap of rock, he saw a head above the wall of the castle, looking toward him. Had he been seen? He could not be sure, but afterward kept well down in bracken and heather. A grove of trees on a rise of ground allowed him to stand and search out the land and to listen for the sound of rushing water. Afar off, he heard a wolf's lonesome howl. He wondered if it could be an evil omen. He smoothed the amber keepsake and hoped the gods would be kind.

He still did not know how he would carry water but hoped that some shell, some hollow stone would come to hand. Then, before leaving the wood, he looked about for a fallen branch to carve with his belt knife. There were many about, and one he found with the center rotted away. It was easy to hollow it to the clean wood for a cup.

When Brus came to the burn, he followed it to where the water was quieter, where deep pools stood hedged about by great stones, and where speckled fish hid and darted. Food! Here was food aplenty. He lay down on a flat stone with his face to the sun so no shadow was cast into the water and reached down carefully. This was not new to him. He had done it many times at home. He cornered a fish among the stones and came up with a wiggling brown trout. The knife quickly quieted it and showed the pink inside meat.

Before leaving the burn, Brus looked about at the flower-decked field which stood high above the green sea. The heaviness in his breast lifted for a time. A feeling of joy took its place. Joy in the freshness of the morning; the provision of water and of food.

He filled the wooden cup. Already he had left his father too long. He went back over the way he had come, keeping out of sight this time after leaving the wood.

He started down the slope to the cavern.

Something froze his blood. Some strangeness. Showing beyond the sharp edge of rock was his father's foot.

How came he out of the cavern? Why lies he there?

A step or two more showed Brus the whole matter.

There lay Harald all quiet and with unmoving limbs, his head among the gray stones, and all covered with moss and lichen; with tiny stonecrop, pink and yellow, violet and blue, "To make a garland for his dying," thought Brus. And all adown the stony place was reddened with his dear blood.

This, then, was the end of the venture: their father dead, their mother lost, Jan captive.

Brus called upon all he had of courage and of endurance, for this was hard to bear; this stillness, this unmoving figure that had been his father, Harald Redbeard, seeing nought of early sun, hearing nought of the song of the skylark.

Where had his father gone? Where could he be buried?

Brus looked about him. Then he bethought him of the cavern. It seemed best to leave him there. There was no place among the rocks and stones to make a grave.

As before, Brus made a sling of his own cloak, for Harald's was not around him and the jewel was gone! So, thought Brus, someone had seen him. Someone wanted the talisman. Who? Perhaps the murderer had been one of the visitors at the feast. Perhaps someone who had known of the jewel. It could not be Bègan Mòr, else he would have seen to it that the jewel was removed before Harald had been thrown over the wall. If only Brus could see Jan, *if he still lived.*

Brus dragged Harald's body slowly up between the rocks and into the cavern where he composed his limbs. He took from his father's belt pouch the box of carved walrus tusk that held the flint tinder.

"No need has Harald Redbeard now for earthly fire. The gods will give heat to warm his bones," thought Brus sorrowfully.

He found the belt knife sticking up out of the floor of the cave, so he placed it on Harald's breast, since there was no shield, no sword, to show that he had died in battle. He stood for a moment, hands clasped, tears flowing, and bade his father —farewell——

Outside the cavern once more, now careless whether or no he be seen, Brus looked about for a standing stone on which he could leave a record of his father's death. He looked up. Was there no comfort, no solace for this weight of stone in his heart? Was there no place for him or for Jan in this land?

All about rose the hills; the hills of Scotland, blue in the morning light. They had stood since the world began, would stand for a thousand years to come. A rush of tears fell from Brus's eyes. He was comforted.

With a smaller stone for hammer and the belt knife he began to carve in runic letters his father's name. He had cut the first three letters,

$$H \vdash R$$

(HAR), wishing he had learned better how to do it, when the sound of voices, of the movement of horses, the clink of harness came to his ears. He stood to see what went forward, but only the top of the castle keep rose above the hill. He crept to the head of the rise. From there he could see a train of people issuing forth from the castle water gate. They came across the pools left on the floor of the sea loch, up the steep bank almost to where Brus crouched among the bracken. He could have reached out and touched the horses' fetlocks.

At the head of the column were heralds bearing the swords of the nobles. Following were Gavin of Lorne and his men; among them, Jan! His bright hair, uncovered, shone in the morning light.

Brus almost shouted, but remembered in time. When the last of the horsemen and those afoot had passed, Brus left the standing stone and the rune and followed them, keeping always out of sight and some way behind. Already he had said, "Farewell" to his father.

As the way led inland, Brus listened for the thunder of horses' hoofs, the clink of harness to guide him, so he need not keep the column in sight. The narrow way led up over hill and dale, cloud-shadowed and deep with heather. Sometimes the sun shone on shepherd's cottage or sheepcote, making a bright spot in the dark landscape.

Sometimes he passed highland cattle which stood on the hills, looking out beneath widespread horns through thick forelocks; sometimes long-faced sheep, tended by one lonely shepherd, fed on the sparse, flower-decked grass. Brus remembered how his father had told them of native sheep and cattle. The remembrance of father and of the home high above the fiord, of mother and the lost ones, was as if a heavy weight lay in his breast. He hurried on to catch a glimpse of Jan, and the sight of his gleaming hair among the others eased the pain of remembering.

Once, when the sun was high and they crossed a burn, the

whole company stopped for water and to rest the ladies and their womenfolk, Brus, seeing them stop, gave the wail of the curlew, followed by the peewee's cheep. Jan lifted his head, knowing Brus was near, for 'twas another sign between them that each knew of the other's presence. Brus saw the bright head go up, and knew he had been heard.

Jan begged leave to go with two young squires to gather wood for a fire and to search for betony to make a brew of mint tea for the Lady Julia, mother of the laird. She complained bitterly of saddle weariness and aching bones.

When leave was given him, he slipped into the grove of trees whence had come the birdcall. Under cover of picking up twigs he glanced under a young oak thicket, and there, as he had hoped, discovered Brus.

A swift embrace and silent exchange of gestures told each a great deal. A questioning look and a sober nod told Jan his father lay dead. A motion of the hand, that the talisman was gone. A rubbing of the middle told Brus that Jan was well fed, and a shake of the head told Jan that Brus was empty. A moment's delay while Brus thrust into Jan's fingers the leathern bag with the amber token, the tinderbox and the spoon, and a few kernels of beech mast he had found. He put his cloak upon Jan's shoulders, clasped his hand, and they exchanged places. Brus became the laird's equerry and Jan the fugitive.

Brus quickly gathered a handful of sticks and stood to answer the call from the young Scots, who had lost sight of their prisoner.

"*Ee-an!*" they shouted, instead of "Yan," the way it had always been said. "*Ee-an!*"

"Here I am!" called Brus. "Here!" And when he had come up to them, neither showed by look or word that Brus had taken Jan's place. When they had gathered sufficient wood and the leaves of betony and returned to camp, Brus served the laird and was not discovered.

All day the horsemen led the company across the isle, and all day Jan followed as Brus had done. Sometimes he saw Brus tall among the young squires. Sometimes the company was lost to sight among the rocks, and Jan must follow as best he could by guess and by what he could hear. He wished he had learned from Brus how it had been with their father. Where did he lie? How had Brus found him? When would he and Brus meet again, and where?

Where the land fell away, Jan saw an old shepherd, who was folding his flock for the night. Beyond, low-lying, was a crofter's cottage, settled into an arm of the hill; its thatched roof down over its window eye, and smoke, blue and thin, curling from a hole in the roof. It was near the day's end. Jan was very hungry, for he had eaten the beech mast long since. Did he dare ask food of the shepherd?

He waited till the company was over the hill and making camp near the sea channel, then rose and went toward the sheepfold.

The shepherd said nought when Jan appeared, but only leaned on his crook and waited for Jan to speak.

"Good even, shepherd," he said. "Is it here that water is low when tide is out, so men may pass over to mainland?"

"Aye," said the shepherd, looking at Jan with narrowed eyes.

"Could food and shelter be had at yon holding?" Jan asked.

"Aye," said the shepherd again. He looked at Jan for a long moment, then went on.

"What of that company lately passed? Saw I not thee among them?"

Jan did not know how he should answer. Then he bethought him of a way not to lie, yet not to tell the shepherd of his twin brother till he could be sure of his friendship.

"Aye," he said, "I was traveling with them." Which was truth.

"Art in thrallage to yon laird?" asked the shepherd.

"Aye," answered Jan. "But I am come thirsting to this holding, and in my country a stranger at the gate is made welcome, if so be he come in friendship."

"What is thy country? How can I know thou'rt a friend?" The shepherd was wary. "In this country, too, a stranger is welcome. Our Lord says, "Be not forgetful to entertain strangers.""

"I come from the North Country," said Jan. "My father brought our long ship to Britain for us to find a new home with the Danes, our kinsmen. But storm drove us here and here broke our ship apart. Then, because one of our warriors flew into rage when Bègan Mòr's men taunted him, they fell upon us and killed all our warriors and my father also, taking me as prisoner to be equerry to his lordship."

Jan almost spoke of Brus, then remembered.

The shepherd nodded his old head knowingly.

" 'Tis Bègan Mòr's way to murder first and question after," he said. " 'Tis like ye were at the feast, then. The feast to bind the young laird and the lady Nineag. Fair is she as the pale field orchis," said the shepherd, "and false is he as Judas, who betrayed our Lord. Black Gavin is Scot, yet hath sworn allegiance to Ethelred, the Saxon King, thinking to find advantage in it. He thinks it secret, but 'tis known. And he hath also given his oath to Malcolm of Scotland. I hold with no traitor. I be Scot!"

"But come." The shepherd led the way down the hill through stony scree and heather to his hut.

62

Peat lay drying by the door, where an old woman met them.

The cottage was snug and warm, and fragrant with peat fire; the rafters low and smoke-blackened, and hung with bunches of herbs drying and scenting the air—just as they had done at home, thought Jan. Wooden bowls held porridge set forth by the old wife, and horn spoons with thistle-carved handles were set beside them. Jan thought of the spoon Fergus had given Brus.

Fergus! He would never see him more! He put away the painful remembrance.

"Christ's blessing on thee, son," the woman greeted him, hanging his cloak beside her husband's. "Thou'rt welcome to our fare."

"Sit down, lad," said the shepherd. Then, before putting spoon to porridge, he closed his eyes, made the sign of the cross on his breast, and said a prayer of thankfulness for food and for life; asking mercy upon those whose lives had been lost by water and by sword, and forgiveness for the murderers.

Jan was very hungry and wished the prayer had been ended, whether it was said to the gods he knew or to that other God he knew not.

When food had been eaten and cleared away, they sat about the table in the long evening light, the woman silent, listening, while her man talked, and while Jan spoke of the tragic ending of their venture. His voice shook with outrage when he told of the massacre of Harald Redbeard, his father, and all his men, and, without his willing it, his saga turned into poetry very like to the way it had gone at the betrothal feast, but he added the slaying of the warriors and his father, chanting the lines to the doleful end.

"I declare vengeance upon the slayer!" he shouted. "Vengeance! And the wrath of the gods! The wicked one shall be sought till he is found! I, my father's son, say it."

"Ssssh!" the shepherd hushed him. "Vengeance is the Lord's. Beware lest ye find that for which ye seek! It can be an evil thing! The Lord says, 'Forgive them as I forgive you.'"

"Is this Lord, then, like one of our gods? Is he like Odin or Thor?" asked Jan.

"There is but one God, lad, and Jesus Christ is His Son. Listen, while I tell ye. 'Tis all told in a holy book, they say, though I canna read. But pilgrims come this way and monks, who go to the holy place of St. Andrew, and who travel about the isle preaching and teaching. I think on these things in the silence of the days and nights when I watch the sheep."

Then Donald spoke of that first Christ Mass when Mary, the gentle Maid, the mother of our Lord, and Joseph, her husband, could find no room in the inn, when they had gone to Bethlehem to be taxed. How the Babe had been born in a manger and the beasts had warmed the shelter with their breath. He told of the Wondrous Star that had appeared in the heavens and had stood over the place where the young Child lay. In his mind Jan could see the wintry sky and the poor shepherds keeping watch over their flocks, lest wolves creep into the fold. He could feel the icy wind, and the wonder of the shepherds at the Star. Excitement ran through him in a shiver as he seemed to hear the choir of angels singing, "Glory to God in the Highest, and on earth, peace. . . ."

What were *angels?* Were they, perhaps, like the Nornir Maidens, those wise-minded ones who, the elders said, soared over the sea? Who helped those in need, especially mothers of children? Jan thought of Mary, the gentle Maid. Was she as fair as Nineag? For she was fair indeed.

64

When Jan came back to himself, Donald was telling of the Christ as a young man and the beginning of His mission; of those disciples who had followed Christ at His bidding; the first, two fishermen, Simon and Andrew, his brother, who had left their nets and followed Him. Andrew was now called St. Andrew because he had suffered death for his belief, outspread upon a cross in Patras, in the first years of the Christians, even as his Lord had suffered and died upon a cross before him.

Donald bent down and made a sign in the ash of the hearth with his finger.

"The cross of St. Andrew was like this ✕ ," he said, "instead of this ✝ , which is the sign of Christ's cross and the one we follow."

"Why," said Jan in wonder, "this sign is very like the token I carry, which we call Thor's hammer. See?" He brought out the amber keepsake and showed it to Donald.

"Aye, 'tis so," agreed Donald, " 'tis very like, only one arm being shorter than the other. 'Tis curious. This be Thor's hammer, ye say?"

"Aye," said Jan. " 'Tis said Thor's hammer strikes the anvil to make thunder when we see lightning."

Donald nodded, wondering. He went on with his tale, telling how Andrew had become the patron saint of Scots, because of many wonders wrought through holy relics, arm and finger bones, preserved since his death, brought to Scotland during the eighth century. Now they were enshrined in a monastery which stood on a treeless, rocky headland of the east coast on the North Sea. Pilgrims came to the shrine from all over, even from Ireland. Pictish and Scottish kings had bowed the knee before the holy relics in homage to the disciple of Christ, who had been faithful unto death.

65

"Memory of St. Andrew's martyrdom strengthens our faith and makes us able to endure hardship and grief, and to know joy that Jesus, the Lamb of God, gave His life for every man. St. Andrew and his brother stood near and heard Jesus called the 'Lamb of God' by John, another disciple. John—the same name as yours, laddie! Only, we say, 'Ian [Ee-an].'

"And though he was called the Lamb of God, He called himself a shepherd, so He was one of us. He said, 'I am the Good Shepherd who giveth His life for the sheep.' And so He did, so He did," said Donald sadly. "I thank God I am a shepherd."

Then Donald told Jan about the Last Supper, when our Lord had shared the cup of wine with His disciples and told them of His coming crucifixion. Tears coursed down the old shepherd's cheeks as he told how one had betrayed Him to the Roman soldiers, so He had been crucified, had lain three days in the tomb, but had risen on the third day to prove to all men that death has no power over them that follow Him and His way.

Jan listened with all his heart. This was a wondrous tale indeed. The shepherd's tale had eased the burden of grief in him. He must tell Brus.

4 Morning brought fog, and rain slashing down in a heavy sheet. Jan had waked before the shepherd and his old wife were stirring, wishing he had something to leave for a token of thanks. He had nothing but the tokens he must keep. He rubbed his fingers over the amber, saying an ancient spell, thinking of Brus, who had taken his place, and hoping for their meeting. A short walk brought him within hearing of the laird's company. The men were already astir, folding tents, gathering gear, making ready for the crossing to the mainland, for they must cross when the tide was out.

Clanking of armor and harness, thudding of hoofs, and men's voices were held close to the ground by the heavy air. Now and again the company could be seen when the mist lifted. Where was Brus? How had he fared? One thing Jan knew, Brus would care well for the laird's horse; better than he himself could do.

Jan followed the train the short distance to the strait, keeping hidden when he could, when rock or gorse gave him cover; sometimes trusting to the fog to hide his shining head.

Near the water he found tall rushes, and he bethought him of a way to mingle with the company and not be discovered. He sat himself down among the reeds and plaited a cap to cover him, for every man in the company, if he had not some manner of head covering, at least had dark hair, except Brus. No head was of the shining brightness that Jan and Brus had, though some were sandy.

Another difference was in the way their legs were clothed. Brus and Jan wore trousers, or *truis*, but the Scots wore their knees bare. Jan slashed his truis above his knees, folding them down and wrapping them snugly with the leathern thongs which kept them close. Now, in a crowd of men, with rain falling, and in the excitement of crossing, who would notice that he was not one of them? He felt undressed with knees bare, but this he must get used to. If he and Brus changed places again—and they would—Brus must get used to bare knees as well. 'Twas the way of dressing in this Scotland.

The last of the company afoot were well into the water and

struggling to cross safely without being swept to sea in the channel. Jan let himself into the freezing waters of the strait.

Among the laird's company near the strait Brus stood with the stallion waiting for the laird to mount. The horse was groomed and harnessed, his mane plaited, his tail clubbed and tied. Rain darkened his silky coat, and mud clung to the polished hoofs, but he still showed careful grooming.

"A handsome beast," said the laird, looking him over. "He shows good care. It may be, young knave, ye'll be worth your salt." He nodded approval of Brus's work, "What's your name?"

"Jan, they call me," answered Brus, remembering in time.

"Ee-an, is it?" repeated Gavin of Lorne, putting the emphasis on the first syllable as the squires had done.

"So be it," thought Brus. "I shall be Ee-an now." He smiled to himself as he thought how he had duped Gavin into thinking him Jan. Serving Gavin Dhu was easy when it included caring for animals; the great charger, the hounds, the falcons.

He thought, "If I please his vanity with a handsome mount, well groomed, he may forget the lad Ee-an is a prisoner. We may learn something of the manner of our father's death and find the stolen talisman." His mouth tightened at the remembrance of all that had befallen. He answered shortly, "Aye, Ee-an." He *must* remember to answer to Jan's name.

The laird mounted and fell in behind the heralds. The ladies, swathed in thick cloaks and veils, were mounted. The troop of men-at-arms and women in waiting followed afoot down the hilly passage to the crossing. They were wet with rain, but would be wetter still when they had crossed the strait.

There was much shouting as the horses and men took to the water. Some missed the shallows and had to swim for it. Some of the gear was lost in the current. Brus kept near to Gavin's charger and landed safe on shore. But where was Jan? Would he follow in time? Would he manage to cross ere the tide was in?

Then Brus reminded himself: "He is a strong swimmer; he is well trained. He is a Viking's son even as I."

Jan, in a half hour's time, sometimes swimming, sometimes finding footage where it was shallow, struggling against the strong current, climbed the bank of the mainland. In the confusion of the landing and ordering of the train Jan was able to separate himself from them, and, when he was well hidden, to signal Brus. He was just in time, whistling the curlew's cry—"Curliew! Curliew!"—for, as Brus lifted his head in answer, the pipers swung into a march and the screeching of their wild music began, shutting out every other sound.

Here, as on the isle, the sky hung low, and lashings of rain churned the earth, and the hills lost themselves in cloud. Jan was not sure that Brus had heard the "curliew curliew," but hoped that Brus knew him to be near. Again, he must try to keep pace with the company by hearing as well as sight, for sometimes he could not see what lay ahead. Often he must keep far behind. There was little cover here. Once he seemed completely lost, and was several hours behind.

He finally found the mountain pass and came down into the remains of a village. Every thatched roof had been burned, every hayrick fire, and the smoking stone walls steamed in the cold drizzle. Everyone seemed to have fled the desolate place,

70

and afar off, Jan could see tiny figures moving on the path beyond.

Over the next hill Jan came up with a straggler from the village. He was carrying a small bundle and held a child by the hand. He looked weary and disheartened. He was smoke-blackened, and the child was ragged and thin. Jan spoke to him and inquired the reason for the burning of the village.

" 'Tis not for aught we did," the poor man answered. " 'Tis only that Gavin Dhu of Lorne was angered when Cam-Ron, sheriff of the Glen, demanded tribute. Gavin would not pay. He and his men attacked the sheriff, drove him off, then set upon the villagers. Black Gavin demanded our allegiance to him that he might claim this country as well as his own. Yet he hath given his oath to the Saxon King, and not a man of us would pledge allegiance to him! WE BE SCOTS!"

"Hath he not his own lands? Is he not lord of Lorne?" asked Jan.

"Aye, he is," agreed the man, "but he is not a true Laird of Lorne, else he would not bow the knee to the Saxon. He is now betrothed to Bègan's daughter, and thinks to make himself one day thane of the isles; then who knows? He may have an eye on the throne! He hopes to make himself strong, too, by taking all that we poor folk own, even as he burned the Pictish fortress in the spring of the year, thinking to make them his vassals. Little he knows them! They fled to the hills, but they bide their time! Let him look to his defense! Let him look to his life! We be all Scots!

"Our village is gone, our crops burned, but still *we be Scots!* The thane of the Glen must give us food and weapons; must help us build again. Black Gavin is murderer and traitor. He bends the knee to the richest lord, though he claims to follow the cross. Let him guard his castle well, and look to his life—for *we be Scots!*"

Jan tried to tell the man that he, too, was enemy to Gavin of Lorne, but there was too much anger in the man for listening. He only kept on saying, with shaking fist, *"We be Scots!"*

Jan went his way, leaving the man still shouting.

Dark hills rose to mountains again. The way led through another pass, through a deep, forested glen. Often there were streams to cross. When they came out on the hills again, crofters' cottages were dotted here and there, lone and dark with rain, and, near them, shepherds with their flocks. For most of the way the road was not hard to follow, for it was worn with centuries of foot travel and went through hill and glen the easiest way.

Toward the end of the first day on the mainland the company skirted the head of a loch and stopped there to camp. Jan made his camp in a poplar thicket. He bent a bow from a branch of young wood and of thong, and sharpened a stick to a point for an arrow, slitting the other end, in which he inserted, to aid the arrow's flight, feathers of water birds which lay about in the thicket. Then he brought down a bird with it and cooked it for his supper, using the flint and tinder to light a fire of twigs and branches. He took off his *truis* and *breacan* and dried them.

Next morning the hoarse cry of a startled loon rose from the shallows of the loch. Jan looked out, for he stood high above the company on a ridge of land that fell away on both sides, yet was hidden from them. He thought to see Brus as he looked down from among the leaves, for he knew the company was on the move. Instead he saw the bird itself rise on slow wings, and knew it was not a signal from Brus, but the loon that had cried out.

Then Jan saw something else. Beyond the laird's company, and hidden from them by the rise of ground, was a band of men. They were too far away for Jan to see clearly, only that they moved stealthily. There was no glint of armor, nor flash on weapon, and they were afoot. Were these the Pictish men? Were they men from another village ravaged by Gavin? How could he warn Brus? There appeared to be almost as many in the band as in Gavin's company, about seventy or eighty men. Now they were nearer, and Jan saw they were armed with bows and arrows.

Jan watched while the distance between the two companies grew shorter. If he did not warn Brus soon, it would be too late. He might be killed! Would the wood dove's cry let Brus know he was in danger?

He cried out once more—"OoOooo! OoOooo! OoOoo! Oo—oo." He peered out, straining to see the bright head among the moving mass of men and horses as they left camp and came up the rise. Then he saw it. Brus threw back his head with a jerky motion, twice.

The rain had stopped, and though there was no sun a glare from thinning clouds brightened the view.

In a few moments the two companies met where the crown of the hill was. Jan saw them stand to each other an instant, each at the alert while challenge was given.

Suddenly, from both sides rose the war cries, crashing through the morning air.

Knowing attention was all at that point for the time, Jan left where he stood, flitting from copse to tree, from rocky outcrop to stony gorse, till he neared the company. Pipes screeched, heralds blew trumpets and thrust high the swords. Horses neighed and stamped, women huddled together at the edge of the wood, while men-at-arms gathered to defend their lords and the savage clansmen drew their bows.

In the tumult Jan saw Brus slip back among the men, purposefully, as if he had been sent upon some errand by Gavin. He made his way openly till he came to the poplar grove where Jan was watching. A low whistle showed Brus where Jan was.

They met and embraced, each exclaiming at the other's soundness, each grasping the other by shoulder, arm testing arm for strength and realness, each knowing the other safe and whole; brother looking into brother's eyes as if looking at himself.

There was no need for hush and quiet. The noise of battle, clash of weapons, cries of men covered the sound of voices. The boys were free to talk as much as they liked.

When the joy of first meeting was past, they sat down in the bracken to speak of how each had fared, Jan to hear in words of how their father had died and of his tomb in the cavern. They spoke of their mother and the hope that she might yet live; of the loss of their men and all their household, and they wept together as honest men do when grief overtakes them.

"Hark, how the battle goes!" said Brus. They listened, hearing great cries, neighing of horses, sound of weapons. It was still safe to talk.

"Are you not hungered?" asked Brus. "The fare was but porridge in camp. We need meat. How was it with you?"

"I fared well," answered Jan, telling of making the bow and arrow, the bird he had brought down and cooked over the fire kindled with the tinderbox. "Are you taken for me? Does the laird call you Ee-an?"

"Aye, he does," said Brus. "None sees that I am another lad than the one they first knew. And I take care to please Gavin

Dhu, though 'tis but a pleasure to groom the handsome stallion, and to care for the falcons. He shall have little to complain of in my service, and already has said the beasts have good care," Brus boasted. "I know he is vain of his beasts as he is vain of himself. I saw him looking into the brass of his shield, admiring his lip beard. Little he knows how I watch him and his weaknesses."

"Vain he is, of a truth," agreed Jan. "The day we set out from the Winged Isle, the whole company nearly missed low tide because Gavin the Black must smear his hair with seal oil ere he bade farewell to the Lady Nineag."

"Hark!" said Brus. "The battle lessens. Cries are farther away. It seems the bowmen are being pursued. Think you they are Pictish men?"

"Aye, half savage they looked, and the soothsayer did tell of Pictish men. I must get back. I shall soon be needed, or rather, *you* will be needed!"

Brus pointed to Jan's bare knees. "Have you turned Scot, then, that you bare your knees?"

"Scot? No! But it helped me to appear so when I crossed the strait with the others."

"I saw you not," said Brus, "though I looked the whole day long. I heard the curlew, but could nowise answer, save by my head jerk, for Gavin kept me at his heels, tightening the belly strap, loosing the bridle, fetching the falcon. I was not even sure you had crossed ere the tide turned." He reached out to grasp Jan's arm again, to know his nearness.

"Quick," he said. "Let us change places. It is my turn to be the one following. Shall I take the tinderbox and the amber token? It was given for the one who waits and watches. Or, shall we go as we are? I like well tending the stallion."

"*I* do very well as I am," said Jan. "You are better than I with the horses. I am clumsy at their harness and fright them with it. I shall keep the tokens."

Brus went back to the care of the stallion and the falcons. It was easier than being the one who waited. As he left the wood, carrying branches, that his errand might seem a true errand, the sound of fighting was away down the hill.

The battle was soon over. The attack of the archers had been swift, but that of the mounted lords with sword and spear, ax and dirk had been more swift and more terrible. The archers fled, leaving behind on the field ten of their number and two of the laird's men.

Brus mingled with those in the rear who were attending the wounded, slipping through to Gavin's side ere he had been missed; taking the laird's horse to feed and cover. After, he busied himself fetching water from a spring nearby, gathering wood, and setting up tents, for they were to stay the night in that place. He even helped to bury the dead and to set up a cairn of stones marking the burial ground.

Then a hunt was ordered, with hawks and hounds, and men with bows and arrows, Gavin Dhu at their head, to find meat.

A great fire was built in the open space before the tents. Meat was cooked and ale casks opened. The smith forged new parts and mended harness. The sumpter horses were relieved of their burdens. The serving-women and their ladies freshened clothing and combed their hair. Oaten cakes were baked on heated stones, a haggis stuffed, and when the feasting was done, Black Gavin called for piping, for the dance of the sword, and for singing.

"Where is yon lad who came with us new from the Winged Isle?" he asked. "Let him come forth now, and let him sing of the battle and the victory! He made a handsome song at the betrothal feast. Let him come forth! What's his name? Ee-an!" he shouted.

Brus was dismayed. Here was something he had not looked for. Jan, or "Ian," as they said now, could weave a tale in song with ease. But Brus had never made a song in his life! Jan had done it for him.

"Ian!" shouted the laird, and the men about repeated it. "I-an! I-an!"

Brus must reply, and quickly. He left off grooming the bay stallion and went forward through the press. As he walked through the clutter of hounds, one rose and followed him. He thought fast as he went—how should he escape discovery? How should he make verses?

When he came before the laird and had made obeisance, he raised himself to standing, still not knowing what he should do. Then he was so moved to anger by what he saw that all concern for the ballad left him. His teeth clenched, blood rose to his face.

On the laird's shoulder, holding in place the length of wool in the way the Scots wore it, was the stolen talisman! Here, then, was his father's murderer!

"Aah!" said the laird, "here is our skylark! To it, now, teller of tales, singer of songs! Tell of the freshened blades, the fleeing foe, and of us the victors!"

Wild anger brought a cry from Brus's throat. He had no thought of what he would say or do, only that opening his throat and letting forth sound would ease him. His cry was as fierce and bloodcurdling as that of the clansmen. When he uttered it, both arms stretched high and in his hand he brandished the belt knife.

Brus keened the thoughts that tumbled out of his heart. And these are the words of it.

> *Ooonu! Oon-ach! a beast, a serpent,*
> *Killer of fathers, stealer of sons!*
> *Cleaver of heads, thief of the Fairest*
> *Forder of channel, builder of duns!*
>
> *Down the crag tumbling, into the hollow*
> *Strewing the heather, red'ning the gorse*
> *Fell Pictish men, by the laird's sword and skene-dhu*
> *Into the hills the rest took their course.*
>
> *Oooonu! Ooooon-ach! let buzzards feast*
> *Let wolves howl by the ash,*
> *Let them tell of betrayal,*
> *Let dogs their teeth gnash!*
>
> *Let magical runes on talisman stolen*
> *Sorrow and death weave,*
> *And troth now be broken!*
>
> *Oooooooonu! Oooooon-ach!*

Brus ended his savage denunciation in a shriek, as he had begun it, awaiting the cold edge of the laird's claymore on his young neck for his insolence.

Instead a shout went up.

"Hai! Hai! The young cock crows!"

Even the laird applauded the ballad. Brus was astonished. Either Gavin did not understand his different speech or he thought Brus of too little account to notice. "Or," Brus thought, "he *wants* to be known as thief and murderer."

He breathed hard, his blood still racing with outrage and

78

anger. But what could he do? He was one, alone, unarmed but for his belt knife.

Even Jan must have heard the wild song and would know it for a challenge, though words were lost in the evening air.

Suddenly it seemed as if he could hear his father's voice, saying, "Be wary, your likeness to Jan can be a weapon." He swallowed his anger. He must get to Jan again. They must plan a way to recover the talisman. They must plot to avenge their father.

These thoughts ran swiftly through his mind while shouting and applause made a great noise. Then he excused himself from the laird's presence.

"The stallion is much sweated and tired from battle," he said. "I have covered him with a cloth but now must care for him."

He went, by the laird's leave, back through the company, cheered as he went by the men, and followed by the great black hound, who seemed to have chosen Brus for his own.

"Have you no master, then?" Brus asked of the animal who clung to his heels. "Shall I call you my own, and give you a name? Black you are, so Black—*Duig*—shall be your name— Duig!" The long, slender beast looked at Brus with slight nods of his head.

"He knows what I say!" thought Brus.

Duig was of the breed used in hunting wolves; Irish wolf-hound, Murdoch the smith said.

For part of the next day they still camped in that place. Jan stayed in the forest grove, hiding in a hollow tree when men came for firewood. Brus, taking Duig, came to him after dark had fallen, with food saved from supper and carried in his purse.

The laird went with falcon and hounds to hunt pheasant

and wild pig, for they needed more fresh meat. Duig coursed with the other hounds, but whenever they were brought to heel, he followed Brus and no other.

When they rested after a chase over crag and scree, Duig put his head in Brus's lap. Brus stroked it and wished he owned the noble beast.

"Whilst I am the laird's equerry, you shall be mine," he whispered. "Will you, then, be faithful to Ian as well? Will you follow him about as you follow me?" And while he said it, Brus could not have told whether or no he wished Duig to be faithful to Ian. Were they not closer than brothers? Were they not almost as one, being twins? Brus looked into the liquid eyes and called the dog by his new name. "Duig," he said, "Duig."

When they returned from the chase, it was Brus who fed and hooded the falcons, mewed them in their own place. Even the peregrine, the laird's own, allowed the hood to be slipped on with never a scratch, and with little beating of wings. Murdoch Gow, the smith, wondered at it.

"It's a way ye have wi' the beasts, lad," he said. "Never was the laird's peregrine so gentle when he's mewed. Never was his horse in so fine fettle. And yon Irish hound, never did he choose a knee to rest on save thine. He was brought here as a pup, and goes well in the chase, but has chosen no master till now. 'Tis a way ye have."

"Aye," Brus nodded, " 'twas ever so."

Ian, for so he shall now be called, kept down among oak shoots when the hunt passed. Once, when a squire parted branches looking for a bird that had been brought to earth, he was sure he had been discovered, but the squire rode on. He was safe.

He and Brus had talked long in the half-dark midnight. Brus had again spoken of their father's murder, and that he now knew the murderer to be Gavin of Lorne.

He told of the song he had made, and how he had put into it all the hatred and anger he had felt.

"*Never* did I make song before," he said. "Always, when the scald put the task to me to make a song, it was you who did it, remember?" They laughed together, remembering. Brus went on.

"When the laird asked for a song, I was fair frighted. I knew not how I should do it. Then, when I saw the token jewel holding his plaid, something—some fury—rose in me. The song came from my throat, I know not how. It came."

"Aye," said Ian, " 'Tis like that with me. At times, I sing from I know not whence. Times, the song sings itself. I know not how." He stroked Duig's head, but the hound kept to himself. He did not put his head in Ian's lap as he had in Brus's.

"Someway we must find to take the jewel," said Brus. "It is our own, now that father is gone. We must avenge him, we who are left. We, his two sons." Brus finished gravely. They clasped hands in silent, solemn agreement.

"Shall it be my turn now?" asked Ian. "Shall I be the laird's equerry?"

"Wait this while," said Brus. "Tomorrow we hunt. The horses and hounds know my hand. By evening, if it chance that I may slip away, you can take place. The laird will want music again. Give him a song such as you can give, for not again could I make a song. I hardly kept my hand from snatching the jewel from his plaid and taking him by the throat."

82

After the hunt, the company resumed its journey. Ian took Brus's place as equerry. Once more Brus was the fugitive in hiding.

They stopped to camp two nights more. Once they camped in the hills beside an inland loch. There was fresh trout and salmon, caught from the rushing burn.

The armorer, Murdoch Gow, apparently saw no difference in Ian's looks, thinking him the same boy who had joined them at Bègan's dun, as indeed he was! But this he did see. Duig no longer followed him about. He saw, too, that when the falcons were cared for, Ian was always somewhere else, and by the second day the stallion's coat looked ungroomed, his mane uncared for.

"Have ye now lost yer way wi' the beasts?" he asked Ian when they stopped for the second night. " 'Twas a rare way ye had wi' them."

Ian didn't know what to say. He must try harder, be cautious in handling Duig, give him bits of meat. . . .

"The laird keeps me busy at many things," he said. "He asks me to put down my songs in runic writing. He asks me to play at draughts with him. These take time." Ian hastened to take the horse's bridle, took extra care in grooming him, and though the animal was restive, he took time to replait his mane and bind his tail so it would not catch briers.

They had been five days on the road from the Winged Isle when they came in sight of Dundugal, the laird's castle. It stood on high ground as did most fortified dwellings, high above the countryside, where all comers could be seen from the top of the keep and foes known ere they came up the rocky way to the gate.

The heralds rode at the head of the column as when they

had begun the journey. Flags and pennants were flying, swords raised, and chargers stepped high. As they were seen coming across the narrow way between firth and loch, the laird's colors went up on the keep. When they reached the gate, it was opened at the laird's command and the company filed into the courtyard.

The castle was very like that of Bègan's dun, though some of the roofs were of slate instead of thatch. Through an arched way a garden could be seen.

"This Thane of Lorne has much power," thought Ian as he looked about. "His castle is more imposing and more finished. Bègan Mòr's is like a wolf's den. Aye, he is like a wolf himself, cruel and bloodthirsty, howling as he kills. This Gavin of Lorne with his silly lip beard is like a wily fox, thieving and killing as he killed our father. But foxes can be caught. Brus and I have outwitted foxes ere this. We shall catch this one. I shall watch and listen. This I can do as well as Brus. I can be wily too."

5 Brus had followed the company closely except when the hills offered no cover. Then, he must go around them to keep out of sight. It was bitterly cold, and Brus shivered with the mist that pearled his cloak. A great mountain was near, still snow-threaded though the time was called summer.

He had managed to see Ian each night during darkness, and each day had been supplied with food from Ian's portion. Ian, in talk with the gillies, had discovered the way they would take and had told it to Brus.

Next to the last day, as they neared the laird's castle, and forded the end of a loch, Brus lost the company and had to ask his way. It was near night; the tops of hills were lost in fog. The curlews cried, doves mourned, gulls screeched. Brus heard every doleful thing and longed for home in Scania, with his mother safe, his father near to guide them all, and Jan—no, Ee-an—*Ian*—knowing his every thought.

He crossed a small stone bridge over a mountain stream. He stood looking down at the roaring water as it gushed over its stony course. A lamb, lost from its mother, was marooned on a rock in the middle of it. Brus, stepping carefully, for the water was very swift and very deep, made his way over the rocks and brought the lamb to safety. Then, looking up, he saw a woman standing not far away, near the door of a crofter's cottage. She was wringing her hands at the plight of the lamb and joyful at its rescue.

"Come into the house," she invited Brus; "only now, when I heard how the roar of the burn had increased, did I see yon lambkin. I heard the ewe bleating, and came to look, but knew no way to get to the rock.

"Sit ye by the fire and I'll bring ye a warm sup of milk. My man is with the thane's company and will no be here tonight. He must go to the castle and do his bit of service first."

When Brus thanked the woman, she remarked his different speech.

" 'Tis no here ye'll belong," she said; "and the fairness of yer skin and hair is like milk and silver, though ye be ruddy

86

enough." She smoothed Brus's cheek with her hand, like his mother had used to do, and his cheek became the more ruddy with the gesture. It was long since a woman's hand had touched him. How long? It seemed like years. Yet, was it so long? A few weeks at most.

He asked the woman what she was called, that he might speak her name as he talked.

"Morag," she said. "Like that of the lazy wife in the old tale." She laughed.

"Will you tell it me, then?" asked Brus. "Will you tell me the tale?"

"Aye," Morag agreed. "While the pot boils and the porridge cooks, I'll tell the tale."

She put peat on the fire, then sat beside Brus with her spindle and twisted yarn as she spun the story.

Brus was weary of watching and waiting, of fearing and following. He sat content.

"Morag, the lazy one," said Morag, the wife, "wished every morning that someone would red up her house and put peat on her fire, for oft her good man came home from the fields and found her sitting by the cold fireplace, ashes all about the floor, the bowls unwashed, the bedplace in a tumble. One day a fairy came and said she would do Morag's work if Morag would bake scones for her and her fairy friends. Morag was delighted. She baked scones that were light and crisp and the fairies ate them all before they were cold. She had hardly finished baking again when the fairies were back begging for more—and *more*—and *more*.

"To be sure, Morag's house was swept in a wink. Her fireplace was never empty of peat. Her bedplace was smooth and tidy. But she had no time for dreaming, no time for lying on the grass in the sun, no time for picking flowers, for the fairy-folk kept begging for more scones and more scones. One day, when the sun was hot, Morag had been baking since early morning when her man had gone to the field. The fairy-one came to her door and asked for scones, and before the scones had been put on the table to cool, they were whisked away, and the fairy was back again for more.

" 'Out of the way! thou greedy one!' shouted Morag. 'No time have I had to breathe or to dream, no time to watch the fireflies, no time to gather field flowers. Begone! I'll attend to my own house!'

"Thereafter, Morag was no longer the lazy wife. She tended her house and kept it tidy. She baked scones for her good man. She kept the peat fire burning, and *it is burning to this day, after a hundred years!* Still Morag had time to help her man tend his flock, to make wool, and to weave." The woman laughed as she finished her tale, and Brus laughed too. "It is good," he thought, "when people laugh together." Then, be the cold as chill as the snow on the mountain, or the mist as heavy as the cloud he wears for a hat, there is warmth in the heart. He wondered if Ian were as warm as he. He wondered if Duig slept close to him and was his friend.

When the porridge was cooked, and Morag and Brus had shared it, she asked him to tell of his home and how he had come to Scotland. Brus told it all, but never did he speak of Ian. That was still their own secret pledge, one to the other. He told simply that he had been lost from the company when they passed through the mountain.

He told of the murder of his father, and his vow to avenge him.

Morag spoke softly, almost to herself, but Brus heard it.

"The Lord will take care of our enemies," Morag whispered, "if we trust Him and bide His time." She looked not to Brus, but into the fire.

"Who is this 'Lord'? Whenever did not sons avenge their father?" Brus asked her angrily.

"*He* is the Gentle One. The Christ, the Son of God," Morag answered him.

"Her face shines," thought Brus. "Yet she knows not our way." He said aloud, "No son leaves his father's death unavenged. And who is this God? We have many gods. We have Odin, the Wise One, Freya, the beautiful, and we have Thor, whose mighty hammer thunders in the storm. Thor is tall as a mountain, his beard is of briers. When he girds on his belt, his strength is doubled. He is a strong god. We have the great Ash, the Tree of Life. It has roots in the ground and its branches uphold the heavens. Yggdrasil is its name. We have Loki, the god of mischief. He draws the grasses from the earth, and then, to cheat the frost giants, he draws them into the earth again. We have many gods."

"Aye," said Morag. "A great tree I know of, but it is the oak, *we* call the *Great Tree*. That is of the old time. In the branches of the oak grows the mistletoe, the plant of the Druids. At the feast of Christ's Mass, we gather it; holly too, and leaves of laurel to deck the house for His birthday. Know you of the Christ Mass?"

"No." Brus shook his head. What was all this talk of a "Christ"?

Morag went on, her eyes looking again into the peat fire, her fingers swiftly twisting the woolen thread.

"Christ Mass comes at the dark of the year, when all is black with cloud and the ground is hard with frost. When the blood freezes with the bitter wind, when flocks and herds shiver in the fold, then comes the Christ Mass. The kirk is bright with candlelight. Then is His Lord's grace kind to us, and we have meat and feasting. Then hear we again the Bethlehem story of the Babe in a manger born." Morag sighed with happy remembrance. "The Christ Mass is a wonderful time."

"If it is the dark of the year, we have that too," said Brus. "We call it Yule. Then extra food is given animals and we, too, have feasting. It is when the wheel of time stops and the sun is gone from our land. Then, when we have made offerings to the gods, the wheel turns again, and we have light. We call it not a Christ Mass. It is Yule."

"Aye," said Morag eagerly. "Yule! We call it that too! Better I like 'Christ Mass.' "

"Yule is good enough for me," said Brus. "Always Harald, my father, saw to it that Yule ale was brewed. Always the feasting was great in our hall, and the fires pushed back the dark." Brus was silent, then, for a time, thinking of Harald, remembering that night on the isle, thinking of finding him beaten and dead; of the jeweled talisman, stolen.

"Harald shall be avenged!" he burst out. "It is for his *sons* to avenge him."

Morag saw that Brus would have none of the Christ story.

"There has been already too much bloodshed," she said, shaking her head. "Ah well, it may be the Lord will take vengeance out of your hands. Come, let you to bed and sleep. Morning brings new thought and fresh courage. Come." She led Brus to a heap of straw in the corner with sheepskin covering it. He wrapped himself in his cloak and slept.

By early light Morag was stirring in the inglenook, and the smell of oat porridge was again in the cottage. There was even a bit of salt to give it flavor. While he ate, Morag told Brus the way he should take to the castle of Gavin, Thane of Lorne.

Morag set Brus on his way with a blessing and a half loaf of bread, making that same sign of the cross Ian had seen the shepherd use; a touching of forehead and breast, a murmur of words.

"You have been kind to a thirsting stranger," said Brus. "My thanks and farewell." He left Morag and went his way, fording the loch head, and on through the hilly way toward the castle where Ian was. Bright yellow lilies grew along the path which followed the high land; figwort, too, spiked the hedgerow and there were thistles that pricked. The day was fine and soon warmth of the sun took chill from the air. Brus carried his cloak on one shoulder as he had seen the Scots do.

Soon after midday he came to a small village. There was a sheep market place where countryfolk had gathered; children and dogs ran in and out among them, and in the center was a stone cross. It was tall and sturdy with a circle enclosing the cross, and carved upon it were runes and interweaving lines like those Brus had always known. They were like the symbols on the stolen jewel. Had these interweaving lines some new meaning, then?

How would he find a way to recover the jeweled token? How would he find Ian, and he within the castle? How could they cross Scotland to the country where the Danes were?

He followed the edge of the loch, as Morag had told him to do, around a bend skirting a rocky hill where sheep grazed. An old ewe looked up as he passed, looking as Father had said, like Einar's old wife, and her "meh-eh-ing" sounded like the same gossip. The company had surely reached the castle long since, for there it stood high above the village, the Thane's colors flying from the keep, showing he was there.

Meantime, when the castle gate had closed and Ian found himself inside with the laird's company, he felt as if a whole world were between him and Brus. He had heard no signal, had seen no sign of Brus since the day before. He must be watchful. He must listen. He must be ready. "Ready for what?" he thought.

He remembered his teaching through childhood. Be ready! Ready for anything. Ready to make friends; ready to meet foes; ready to escape danger. Ready!

These thoughts kept Ian busy while the company assorted itself. Ian stabled the charger and fed him, then watered him from the well in the courtyard, and cleaned his coat. " 'Tis not as Brus would have done it," he thought, "but well enough!" Duig wandered into the stall and lay down, but didn't first come to Ian as he would have to Brus. When Ian gave him water, he wagged his tail and was not unfriendly.

Supper in the hall brought the company together again. Some of the nobles had already left the troop to take their own roads, west or south. The thralls, who were not in regular attendance at the castle, had gone to their homes.

New faces were at table where the high seat was, among them a boy of twelve and a man in monkish garb. Before bread was broken, he rose and blessed the company, making the sign on breast and forehead as had the first monk and the shepherds. Every man and woman in the hall made the sign as well.

"This must be a powerful spell!" thought Ian. "This Lord must be a strong god!" Ian went through the motions as best he could.

92

When it was time for piping and for sagas, the soothsayer added to his tale the story of the journey home from the isles and the encounter with the Pictish men. He mourned the two men they had lost and spoke of the swift death meted out to the enemy.

When he sat down, Black Gavin called for another tale.

"Let the youthling come forth!" he cried. "Let *him* tell of the battle. His tale will have a more lusty ring, for never have I heard so fierce a tale as his. Hear you now, sirs, does Black Gavin keep his lands. Hear you! And know that I, who inherit this country of Lorne, am no weakling! *Hear you* how this young cock crows!"

Ian, as Brus had been, was caught unaware. How could he make a song like Brus had made? How *could* he? All Ian's songs had been of other things, sad, when sadness was in him, but not fierce and terrible as Brus's song had been.

He came forward, threading his way, not knowing what he would say, or what song he should sing. As he neared the high seat, the laird called out to him, laughing at him as Bègan Mòr had done, taunting him for youth and weakness.

Ian saw the brooch clasping his plaid, saw it gleam in fire-light.

His blood rose. Black Gavin shouted at him, "Hah!" He said, "This is the eaglet! This pale-haired *Norsir!* This downy-cheeked warrior. He has come to take our land with nought but a belt knife. This orphaned one! Harken now, while the eaglet keens his battle song!"

That was enough.

Ian's blood boiled. His teeth bared. He clenched his jaw and grasped his belt knife. He raised it on high while he roared forth the challenge. He began, as Brus had done with the

93

ancient battle cry. It shrieked to the roof and echoed on the stones.

Oooooonu! Ooooooon-Ach!!

Bègan, the wolf, unfriended the eaglet,
   Black Gavin, the fox, Red Harald hath slain,
Hath stolen the token, his dear head hath broken,
   Among the cold stones his body hath lain.

Through village and townlet the fox took his way,
   Burned hayrick and cowshed, cottage and barn,
Wife, child, and husband laid limp on the greensward,
   The fox from their bodies their dear life has torn.

On hill where the deer feed, the Pictish men fought,
   with arrow and longbow defended the knob,
The fox threw the spear, the dirk killed those near
   With broadsword and skean-dhu, their lives he did rob.

"Where lies the slinky fox? Where is his lair?
   His eyes shall the eagles pluck, leaving his hair.
Where lies the eaglet now, where oh, where?
   He waits for the sly fox, this youthling, so fair——"

Ian stopped for breath, his heart beating wildly, expecting, like Brus, to be cut down. Hearing with wonder the loud applause! They must be daft! Did they not understand? This song had been a challenge to an enemy, and they laughed at him!

"Ooooooonu! Oooon-ach!" he shrieked.

He was blind with anger as he made a stiff obeisance, turned on his heel, and went back to the stable. The horses and the gillies were his friends, at least. He threw himself upon Duig, and shook with the anger that was in him.

94

Murdoch found him there when he came to feed the dogs. He put his hand on Ian's shoulder.

"Grieve not, gentle lad," he said. "Thou'rt but in the flower of thy youth and may have yet a free life. Thou'rt in thrallage now, but we, the carls, the serfs, may be in thrall our lives long. This laird, who now this land doth hold, is cruel and sly. Ye need not be told. We wait a kinder one, as was the laird who had this land before, Dugal of Lorne. We pray and hope that a better time will come. Let us complain to God above that He will remember us in this plight. For He sent His Son, Who died upon a tree that the poor and meek might live, the same as He."

Ian looked up at Murdoch.

"Are you, then, Black Gavin's enemy too?" he asked in wonder.

"His enemy and his thrall; all one. Compelled to serve him, hating him, whiles. Yet hating *him* not, for our Lord says, 'Love thine enemies,' but hating the deeds he does."

"Why do you not kill him?" asked Ian. "You are strong."

"I am but one among many who think not as I do, and I am not a killer. I am a smithy," said Murdoch. "When he spoils the earth and takes for himself and his men-at-arms whatever comes his way, some *like* the way of it. I like it not. I bide with him—waiting. . . . He took me prisoner, burned my croft, killed my wife and children. If I killed him, another like him would take his place, for they are a powerful lot, these. And I like not killing. I bide. I listen and learn, and wait till the Lord gives us a leader and takes vengeance!"

"How can this Lord, whose sign you make, be powerful if He helps you not?" Ian asked curiously.

"In His good time, He *will* help us," said Murdoch. "Perhaps He is helping us now, though we see it not. God's ways are not our ways. We must have faith, for even when all seems against us, all seems lost, we later find that all was for the best. Sometimes one must lose that many others may gain, even as Christ gave His life for us all. We must have faith. Mind you of St. Andrew, who is the patron of the Scots?"

"I know not much of him," said Ian.

"He is the first of those who followed Jesus the Christ. He was a fisherman, and, like many who live hereabout, depended upon the fishing for his livelihood. One night, when he and his brother and the others had fished all night and caught nothing, they saw the Christ walking on the shore in the morning light. They heard Him call to them whether they had any meat, and when they answered Him, 'None,' He called to them to let down their net on the other side of the boat. When they had obeyed, the fish came into the net in such numbers they could scarce lift it. It may be we need to cast our net some other way. We have a good King now, but he has not yet made one country of Scotland. Something may come about that will secure it for King Malcolm and for us. What, we cannot yet see. He is a Christian king, and may be the leader for whom we seek. Time and faith will tell if we follow the sign of the cross."

"Why does this Gavin make the sign then, when he is cruel as *I* know he is? He seems to *like* being thought cruel. Why makes he the sign? asked Ian again.

"There are those who make the sign of the cross, those who speak the name of the Christ, the Holy One, in lip service only, the same as Black Gavin gives allegiance and means not a word of it. It suits him to appear devout, because he is vassal to King Ethelred, and none may be favored by that weak and unsteady young Saxon, Ethelred, unless he call himself Christian."

"If Ethelred be weak and unsteady, why does Black Gavin

swear allegiance to him? Why not to King Malcolm?" Ian was puzzled. It was very confusing.

"Ethelred hath powerful men in his vassalage. They try to reclaim Lothian and all that country between the Tees and the Tweed, for Ethelred. Each one hopes for reward for himself. Once, the Saxon kings fought for Lothian and conquered it, but King Kenneth brought it back to Scotland. Lothian belongs to the Scots. 'Twas ever so. They won it from the Picts."

This did not seem strange to Ian, for it had always been so. Men fought for what they wanted. But never did Harald's men make the sign of peace and then kill and burn innocents and turn traitors.

Murdoch went on explaining.

"If Black Gavin can win Lothian, that country round about Edin's Boro, with help from Ethelred's nobles, he hopes to gain it for himself, and perhaps have the golden circlet set upon his own head. Already, he and his nobles, Bègan and the others, own half of Scotland. If he gains Lothian and is rewarded by an earldom in Northumbria where the Danes are, he may sit in Edin's Boro Castle yet! *He might even be king!*"

"Could you not escape and raise an army of your own, you Scots? We—I meant to say, *I*—would join you! Black Gavin is my enemy too." Ian caught himself just in time. He must not tell about Brus yet, though Murdoch was his friend.

"Ye are brave for a lad so young. We be too poor in men and arms," said Murdoch sadly. "We have no horses, and many be frighted, and durst not say they are for Malcolm. I bide. Times, I hear how they plot and scheme. They think me stupid or deaf. I am neither, though I have no tutoring. I bide." Murdoch nodded his grizzled head. "I bide," he said again; taking a saddle to be mended, he went.

98

Murdoch had barely gone when a young lad came into the stable, the boy Ian had noticed at supper.

"God's grace to you, young friend from the north," he greeted Ian. "For now I know that friend ye are, that ye stand so strong and brave before blackhearted Gavin."

Ian was so surprised at sight of the boy and at his greeting he stood with mouth half open, staring for a moment, before he recovered himself to answer.

"I am glad of our meeting, if so be we are friends," said Ian finally. "I thought to find here only foes." He stretched forth his hand, and the boy, advancing, clasped it in his own.

"I am Alan MacDugal, son of Dugal. Black Gavin is my uncle."

"Yet, he is your enemy?" asked Ian.

"Of all Scotland, he is my worst enemy," answered Alan.

"Then why stay you here in his castle? Are you prisoner to him?"

"Aye, prisoner," said Alan bitterly, "though he says he 'protects' me. Black Gavin killed my father, keeps my mother imprisoned, has stolen our lands, and set himself up Thane of Lorne. Is he my enemy? He tells a tale of how my father's horse stumbled and threw him over a cliff. But 'tis known the tale is a lie. 'Tis known *Black Gavin killed my father* by crowding him over the cliff."

"He killed *my* father too!" Ian held forth his hand again.

Alan clasped it once more. Each knew it was a sign of sworn friendship. Had they not a common enemy? Were they not both prisoners of Gavin of Lorne?

While their hands were still clasped, the loon's cry came through the evening air. Ian heard it. Was it Brus signaling? Or was it the loon as before?

Ian made excuse of care for the stallion and tossed a few straws out the wind hole as he passed. If Brus were near, he might see the straws floating down from such an unlikely place. It was the only reply Ian could make.

He sat down beside Alan to get acquainted.

This same day Brus neared the height where the castle was, and looked about to see what manner of place he could find in which to hide until he could reach Ian's ear. A wood thickened just near the meadow where sheep fed. He went into it, and had not gone far when he came to a shepherd's cottage. The door stood ajar. Brus knocked. A child came to the opening, and a voice called from within.

"Is it you again, then, MacCrone, Big Nose?" The voice came near as the woman who had spoken rose from her loom and came to the door. The child only stood by.

"Oh," she said, seeing Brus instead of the beggar she had expected. "Who is it, then?"

"I am Brus, son of Harald Redbeard of the North Country," said Brus. "I am thirsting. Have you water near?"

Seeing Brus was but a lad, the woman asked him to come in.

"There is water here in the wee jar. Tomas goes to the spring in the morn, so 'tis fresh enough. Ye be no from these parts. I can tell fra yer speaking." Brus laughed.

"Aye, 'tis a long way from my home to the Winged Isle, where our ship was wrecked," said Brus, "and a long walk from there to here. I go to the country of the Danes, where my kinsman is. Is it far from here?"

The woman looked puzzled.

"The Danes? Aye, I've heard of them." Then she became alarmed. "But I've heard no good of them! The Danes are killers and burners!" she cried. "Awa' wi' ye! Awa' wi' ye!" She began pushing Brus toward the door.

"Nay," said Brus. "I am no killer! Besides, *I* am not Dane; I am Norse, and I am but one, looking for shelter and food. Yon laird, *he is* the burner, the harrier, the murderer! He killed my father, and I saw a smoking village he had burned!" Now, remembering, he cared not whether or no he endangered himself by speaking out. "Be you friend to this killer?" he ended.

The woman was too canny to give herself away.

"My man is shepherd in the laird's domain," she said. " 'Tis our living." She took the child into her skirts as if Brus might injure him with a touch.

"Have no fear of me," said Brus. "No harm shall come to you because of me, neither through me nor my kinsman, nor through Black Gavin, though he is my enemy. You have given me to drink. My thanks." He was about to leave and search for other shelter till he could find a way to reach Ian, when the woman touched his arm.

"Stay," she said. "The look of truth is in ye. Ye're but a lad and no such a danger after all. My service to ye." She made a dip with her knee to Brus, as Egil, his mother's bondwoman, might have done. He sat down on the bench the woman brought forward, took of food she offered, and rested, while she went back to the loom and the web of cloth she was weaving.

"If ye would stay for a bit to rest here, to find your way, like, 'tis welcome ye are. 'Tis little we have, a bit porridge, a few roots my man grows, an egg now and then, but our Lord bids us share what we have." The woman made a swift motion across her breast and forehead, even while she passed the shuttle with her left hand.

"There it is again," thought Brus, "that sign. What can it mean?" But he was content to rest his bones, once more, to ready himself for what should follow.

He began to question the shepherd's wife about the castle. Did her man ever enter the gate?

"Aye, times, he must give account of the sheep. Once a month it is, when the moon is new," she said.

"Is it near time for the new moon now?" asked Brus. "So much fog and rain, the storms, and all dire happenings have lost me the moon. Where it should be on this night I know not. It is long since the moon goddess has shown herself."

"We've had much rain," said Una. "A week from this night a new moon will rise over the loch. It being summer, and the sun so late in setting, it can hardly be seen, but 'tis there. A new sickle to shear the grass of the heavenly fields. But each new moon brings us nearer to winter cold. We have a saying: 'At the end of the first week of August's month, winter is born.' " Una ended sadly, thinking of the bitter cold to come, the hunger, the long gray days.

"A whole week to wait?" thought Brus. "A week of seven days and nights, not knowing what goes forth?"

Yet how else could he enter the castle? The walls were very high and rose above a steep cliff from this side. Perhaps from the other it would offer some way of entrance. He would see when night fell. Brus spoke to Una.

"If I may give service to you, I shall do it," he said. "Where is peat for the fire that I may bring it? Or water? I have drunk of what you had. Shall Tomas show me where I may find more?"

"Aye," said Una. "I should take it as a kindness. Go, laddie.

Show Brus where water is. Peat ye'll find near enough. 'Tis only outside the door."

Up through the wooded hill Tomas took Brus. As he went, Brus thought of what he should do. If so be that the shepherd would let him stay, he would find them meat. There must be deer about, hare, and small birds. He began to think of ways to snare them. He would make a bow; he would shape arrows. Let Black Gavin think no one dared take game from the forest. The gods gave food for all! He, Brus, would take food for the shepherd and his wife, for Tomas, and himself.

That first night in the castle, when Ian had discovered Alan MacDugal was his friend, that he and Alan had equal cause to hate Black Gavin, he almost told the boy of Brus. Almost, but not quite. "Let be," he thought; "it can be told later, when Brus and I have agreed to tell it." Yet he felt sure of Alan's faithfulness, for there was a look in his clear eyes, a sureness in the way he spoke.

"I like fine the songs you sing," said Alan. "I have a harp given me by my mother. Shall we then sing and play together?"

"Aye, together, as soon as may be," Ian said. "It suits me well to sing with the harp. Though not for long have I heard it. Once I saw and heard the harp. I was asked by the King of Norway to make a song with it. It went well."

"Come you, then, when all is done here. We shall make music. First, I go to say a prayer to God in the chapel for my mother's safety. You will find me there." He went out of the stable, leaving Ian wondering. Could he, Ian, make a prayer to Alan's God, for the safety of his own mother? His and Brus's? He went about his work, thinking, as he spread straw for the stallion's bed, as he filled the manger with hay from the mow above. He thought he remembered the tale Donald had told him of the Babe born in a manger.

He stepped around the wolfhound, who sought the warmth of the stall, for a chill wind blew.

"Who is this God? What is the spell made by crossing the breast and touching the forehead, whispering words?"

The chapel was small and built of stone. It was cold, but at one end was an altar somewhat like the kind of altar Ian had known in Norway; an altar where sacrifice had been burned to appease the gods, because of a sickness that had swept through the land. He remembered little of it except the smell of burning, an evil smell.

Alan rose from his knees, and took Ian with him to his own quarters; a chamber set along the castle wall where one of the towers stood. It was open to the cold wind where an arrow slit let in a little evening light. Skins covered the bed of boughs in one corner and against the wall stood a prayer stool. Over it was a rood, a cross—two smooth sticks fitted together. Nearby stood the little harp. It was as high as Ian's belt, a lovely shape with carved designs on the polished wood, and where the two parts met at the top was a woman's head, crowned. Alan lifted it and sat on the bed place. He plucked the strings and sad melody came forth. Alan sang his song first, verses and melody sounding like sadness itself, Ian thought.

When it was Ian's turn to sing, he tried to make his song a remembrance of happier time; time when all was well, and he and Brus were together, always. He sang of the meet when all the youths of the district had contested in feats of strength,

when they had raced each other up the mountain steep, when
Brus had made so brave a stand with the Earl's son: when Ian
had sent his arrow flying so true. Into the song he put all his
thought of home, the gathering around the fire, the feasting,
the joy of welcome given Harald when he returned from
voyaging. The fierce happiness of all homely things; their
mother's quiet smile, her care for their comfort. It was a happy
song, but came near to being a sad one, like Alan's.

Then Ian realized he had spoken of his brother, Brus.

Alan said, "That was a fine song. It had much happiness in
it. Who is Brus? Have you a brother, then?"

What could Ian say? He must not betray Brus. He thought
of Bran and Hardi.

"Two brothers I had who went a-Viking, and never
returned," he said.

"And so it was," he thought. "Bran and Hardi were as truly
my brothers as Brus, though not so close."

Perhaps soon Alan could share his secret, but he must wait
for Brus's consent to tell him.

Each day in the castle Ian wondered about Brus and how
he fared. Where did he hide himself? How passed he his days?
Had he found friends, as Ian had? Brus was strong, stronger
even than himself. Perhaps he fared well.

All through the seven days till the new moon Ian and Alan
kept their friendship secret, lest it be noticed by Black Gavin.

"My uncle would suspect us of a plot if he should know we
two are friends," advised Alan. "We who have been orphaned
through him. So let us be strangers when we meet in his company. Murdoch Gow I fear not. He holds his tongue. He it is
who told me truth about my father's death. But some there
be among the men whom I dare not trust."

106

When the laird's company went a-hawking, Ian kept apart from Alan. When they hunted the deer, and sometimes happened near each other, Ian spoke to Alan if need came, but with reserve, as an equerry to his laird's nephew. On days of rain they sometimes met in the stable, sometimes talked in Alan's wall chamber or made music. In the monk's cell they carved rune letters while the monk told them tales of the Christ, or of holy pilgrims. At times, they practiced archery in the long gallery.

Each evening, when all gathered in the hall for supper, Ian longed to snatch the jewel Black Gavin often wore. Each day he thought of ways in which it might be done. When Gavin's drinking horn had been emptied many times, and the Fox half shut his eyes, as if he might sleep, Ian thought the time had come. But always guests were at table, or guards were close keeping watch, or it chanced that he wore some other clasp on his plaid.

Guests were powerful border lords, Ethelred's men, or Scots earls, known by their Highland dress, their burred speech. Always it fell out that the "Southron," or English, came at a different time than the Scots, though once they nearly met. The English came only an hour or so after the Scots company had gone off into the hills.

Once, near the week's end, Ian was commanded to fetch the stallion and accompany the laird when he sallied forth at nightfall. He and Black Gavin went alone. Ian rode the mare.

They traveled several miles toward the south where the charger was left in Ian's care. Gavin went to a wooded place where he met certain others, Englishmen, as near as Ian could make out in the failing light, for none wore the plaid or bonnet of the Scots.

On the return to Dundugal, Ian was near to recovery of the jewel, near to making an end of the Black Fox.

Gavin seemed lost in thought. "Or," thought Ian, "in scheming." He said little, only "Stay" when they crossed a stream. He dismounted, and knelt to drink from it. Seeing his dark image reflected in the water dimly, he arranged his plaid, smoothed his lip beard. "Vain creature," thought Ian, sitting, waiting.

For an instant, as he rose from drinking, Black Gavin stood beneath Ian, near as his hand, *near as the knife in his belt!*

He grasped it and half withdrew it.

He hesitated. It was a coward's way to kill an enemy from the back. Yet, what honor kept Black Gavin from ravaging the countryside, from orphaning children?

While Ian hesitated, the moment passed. Black Gavin lived, not guessing how near he had come to death at his equerry's hand. Familiarity had dulled his awareness of Ian, as familiarity with killing and burning had dulled any mercy in him.

Ian loosed his tensed muscles, quieted his fast-beating heart. He followed Black Gavin through wood, over hill and through glen, up the steep approach to the gate, over the drawbridge, back into the castle.

He might have gone free! He might have found Brus! He might have killed his enemy!

Yet he was still prisoner. Why had he returned?

He remembered Alan MacDugal was prisoner as well.

6 When Gregory, the shepherd, came home to find Brus there, he looked questioningly at him but said nought. Una, his wife, set his supper before him as she made Brus known to him.

"Let be, Greg," she said. "This lad was hungered and I fed him."

Still Gregory said nothing, but looked Brus up and down, seeing his fair hair and skin, his cloak of red wool, his blue kirtle, his cut-down *truis*. Brus awaited his welcome. Finally Gregory spoke.

"Ye'll be Norse, eh, lad?" he said. "And yer name?"

"Aye, Norse," said Brus, "son of Harald Redbeard."

"Brus MacHarald, is it?" Gregory nodded as he caught a corner of Brus's mantle and rubbed it between his fingers. "Good cloth is in yer cloak and kirtle, but no so firm as yon that webs the loom. How come ye here, alone?"

Brus told again his story.

"We came in peace, said Brus, "to settle with our mother's kinsman, Heming the Dane, where he has a holding near Scald Thorp on the east coast."

"What seek ye here in the country of Lorne?"

"I have cause to think Gavin of Lorne or one of his men killed my father. I seek him," Brus answered. "I seek a way to enter yon castle, and ask your help. Silver I have none, nor treasure. But I have a strong arm and a sure eye, and am no stranger to hunting."

"We are but poor folk, with scarce enough to feed our own. Black Gavin sees to that. He takes what he wants wherever he finds it, and cares not that our stomachs stick to our backbones, that our knees shake, that our heads spin from hunger. A sheep at Christ Mass, aye, and Yule ale; a feast when harvests are gathered; those he gives of his bounty." Gregory spoke bitterly. "Most times, he keeps close watch on every bit of food. Spies be set to watch streams that none of the laird's fish be netted, none of his deer slain; no sheep slaughtered save for the laird's table. Tallies must be cut on sticks, showing the yield of lambs, the weight of shearings."

Then Gregory shrugged his shoulders, lifting his brows, half closing his eyes; scratching his chin.

"Times, now, a lamb falls from a cliff, times, wolves raid the fold, and times, eagles swoop down. Not often, not often. Black Gavin believes what he *sees,* and hardly that!"

"Can you not rise against him? Take his lands and keep them for those who till them?" asked Brus.

Gregory shook his head.

"Not yet, though the time is not far off. Many follow Black Gavin for the glory of it; the sound of the pipes, the spoil he *promises,* though he gives it not. When Dugal, his elder brother was Thane, things went better. A bit of meat found its way into the pot, whiles; a salmon or trout, once in a way."

Brus nodded. Dare he tell the shepherd that Ian was within the castle? That Ian was his brother, his twin? Should he speak of the jewel Black Gavin wore as his own? He would wait.

"Let me go with you when the tallies are taken," he said. "Give me some cover and a shepherd's crook, such as you carry. Let it be that I am your kinsman."

"Aye," said Gregory, "if ye will. Think ye to blast the castle wi' ye'r own two hands?"

Brus thought a moment before answering. If he should enter the castle with Gregory, Ian might be there in plain view. Gregory would know of his twinship; keeping silence would be of no avail. He *must* tell.

"I have said, 'I am alone,' and so it is, yet is not. My brother, *I*an they call him, though we say Jan, is with Black Gavin, taken prisoner on the isle that dark summer eve. He is my twin. We are like as two herring, one to another. We stay apart, as Harald, our father, bade us, for a weapon, a tool, whereby one may save the other, and for better chance to reach our enemy.

112

We have a vow between us to keep this secret. Let it be secret still. You I must tell, for it will be discovered when the tallies are taken."

"A-ha! So, 'tis that! And what *do* ye there? Think ye to shake Black Gavin by the hair of his lip as a dog shakes a rat? Ye're a fine braw lad, and ye be two, so much the better. But ye'r no smart enough for yon laird, if ye think to take him in his own castle. Belike ye'll take service with him, eh? If 'tis adventure ye seek, he's yer man!" Gregory laughed shortly. " 'Tis known hereabout that Black Gavin lets *no man* stand in his way; *not even his own brother.* Ah well, come wi' me if ye choose. 'Tis no matter. But 'tis no for a week yet that I go, mind ye."

Brus nodded. Had he betrayed Ian? Would Duig have made friends with him? Would Duig have forgotten Brus?

How should he pass the time? How keep himself unknown as a stranger in the countryside? Of this he spoke.

"We'll make a proper Scot of ye," said Una. "Ye'll pass when I've done wi' ye."

She took from the chest an ancient, threadbare plaid, hung it on Brus's shoulder, and put his own in its place in the chest. Gregory nodded approval, and set on Brus's head a Scots bonnet to cover his hair. He showed Brus how to drape the plaid, over one shoulder and under one arm.

"Ye'll know 'tis fine goods we make, lad," he said. "This plaidie was my father's. 'Twas loomed on yon beam fifty years ago." He motioned toward the loom where Una had sat all day. "The brown is from the heather. A bit of the juice would cover the fairness of thy skin, and dim the bright hair."

Una fetched the dye pot from the shed, and together they made a Scots shepherd of Brus.

" 'Tis like they'll think him brother John's lad," said Una.

"Aye, him wearing the plaid and a'," agreed Gregory. "Be ye a good shepherd? Are ye good with the dogs?"

"Dogs I like well," said Brus. "All animals are kin to me, and answer well to my keeping."

There was good feeling among them, the young shepherd, Una his wife, and Brus the Norseman. Tomas, the wee Scot, had gone to sleep on the pile of sheepskins in the corner.

When dark had fallen, Brus took the road again to survey the castle. He found but one way to enter; through the gate over the moat. The castle was built like a shield, for it had but three sides around it, with a tower at each corner. But one tower was double, so wide and deep that the gate was between the two parts, and there was depth enough for a room over it, where there was a portcullis, and a drawbridge strong and well made. The walls were firm and high and the moat around two sides of the castle was filled to the brim. In one place where the wall rose sheer from the wood there was a windhole. Brus stood close under the wall, and, lifting his head, gave forth the cry of the loon. He waited, but heard only the pacing of the guard on the wall. He kept his gaze on the opening far above, hoping that by some chance Ian might be near, might hear him. He looked till his neck ached, but heard no sound. Only a few pieces of straw came fluttering down. Had Ian dropped them? Had he heard? Brus waited to see if some further token should give proof he had been heard, but the black hole only stared up at the sky.

"I could swim the ditch," thought Brus, "but there is no way to get up the wall, no handhold, no footing."

Brus knew he must be patient. He must wait for the new moon.

114

All the days between, to the rising of the new moon, Una's table was weighted with unaccustomed food. Hares went into the pot, pheasant fell from their flight when Brus's arrow found them. Fish from the loch made a Friday feast.

When Gregory blessed the food before eating, he asked a special blessing upon Brus, saying:

"Bless this wayfarer, the lad Brus who hath furnished our table this while, and hath brought us this gift from the loch for food; St. Andrew be his friend and companion, who was also a fisherman. Amen."

When the food was eaten, Tomas asleep in his corner, the others sat by the fire, and Brus asked for a story such as Morag had told him that night.

"Was this St. Andrew a Scot, then?" he asked. "Tell of him, if he was a fisherman, and tell why he should be my friend."

Gregory began the stories of the saints and disciples who had followed Jesus the Christ; of Andrew the fisherman, and Simon Peter, his brother. He told of the press of people who had followed Jesus to hear His words, how He told them to love one another, and to return good for evil, and how Jesus had to get into a ship to keep from being crowded into the sea; how, when evening had come, and Jesus and His disciples had set forth in the ship, a great storm of wind had risen and filled the ship with water, so the disciples were afraid. They woke Jesus, Who slept in the hinder part of the ship, and He with a word calmed the storm and stilled the waves.

"Ye'll know what the storm was like, lad, having been to sea and been wrecked on the isle."

"Your Christ is valiant, and 'tis a noble story, Gregory," said Brus. "But the sea gods stirred up a fury of wave and storm that wrecked our ship, and it was not stilled."

"Who shall say that ye were not sent here for a purpose?" asked Gregory. "I be but a shepherd, and know these things only by hearing the holy pilgrims tell of them, but I know them to be true, though I know not the reason for the way things happen. We can only hope and believe, for often good cometh of seeming evil, as the lily grows from the slime and dung which feeds it."

Brus nodded though he could not understand.

The week went by on wings. Tomas became Brus's shadow, and never once cried in his mother's skirts.

But Una knew not how to cover the fragrance of cooking that issued from her fire. MacCrone, the beggar, knocked at her door one day and asked of her to satisfy the hunger he had.

"Meat, is it," he said, sniffing, not asking, but saying, for the odors of stewing hare mingled with betony and marjoram, with thyme and wild onion was more than a man could bear.

Una held her finger to her lips. She must feed him, else he would spread it abroad that meat was cooking over her fire; the news might reach the laird's ear.

"Sssh!" she whispered, bidding him enter. "Can it be helped if a hawk seize a hare or if an eagle attack the hawk, and they drop the hare—both? 'Twould be pity not to use the food the Lord provides." She crossed herself.

"Indeed, indeed," agreed the beggar, caring only that his own stomach be filled.

The week was over. The new moon rose over the loch.

"This night," said Una to Brus when he came from the spring with Tomas, "the good man goes with the tally to Black Gavin. Sorry for him if 'tis not a true tally, for Black Gavin knows every ewe that's lambed. Sorry for us all, too, if any whiff of this week's cooking has reached the laird's nose! But, no. Had he heard aught, there would have been somewhat done long since."

When the shepherd and Brus came into the courtyard of the castle, Ian stood near the well with Alan. Duig and the other hounds stood about, lapping the water Ian had drawn for them.

Before Ian realized that Brus was near, Duig had left the bowl of water and had run toward Brus, his tail awag. Short, sharp barks of joy showed his recognition of Brus, even though Brus's face was smeared with heather dye, his bright head covered with a bonnet.

Brus tried to push him away, to ignore him, though he longed to touch the grizzled head. Alan, too, saw how the dog had run to Brus. He thought little of it, for the shepherd came often to the castle, and sometimes had a lad with him.

Ian knew. Ian knew it was Brus. No plaid or ragged bonnet could hide that shape that was as his own, that tallness that was a part of himself, that strong right hand, even though the hand carried a shepherd's crook and the ruddy cheeks were smeared with brown. Yet in no way did he betray his joy at seeing Brus within the stronghold.

He made an excuse to Alan, saying he must carry water to the stallion and bed him for the night. He drew fresh water from the well, walked slowly with it toward the stable, hoping Brus would find a way to leave the others and meet him there.

The shepherd was taken into the keep to give his account to Black Gavin. Alan followed.

Brus made no answer when one of the carls asked him a

question, fearing his speech would betray him. He shook his head as if unable to speak, and muttered foolishly.

"Deaf, is it, ye are?" asked the carl, "or silly? One or the other." He went off.

Brus edged toward the stable, and when no one was watching, slipped through the doorway and along the passage till he came to Ian.

Their greeting was silent. But their looks and actions spoke for them.

Ian pointed with silent laughter at Brus's shepherd guise. Brus pointed, too, at Ian, laughing at his being forced to care for Black Gavin's horses, to do all manner of things he had always hated doing. Their laughter grew so great they were fit to burst if they might not speak. Part of it was the joy in meeting.

Duig followed Brus, and stood close to him, while the boys talked without speaking. The hound tucked his head into Brus's hand.

When all went as usual in the courtyard, and no one came into the stable, they spoke in low voices.

"Heard you the signal when I made the cry of the loon?"

"Aye, I heard," said Ian, "but I was not alone. I could only toss out the straw. Saw you the straw?"

"I saw the bits of straw," whispered Brus, "but could only guess you had dropped them. Stay we as we are, or shall it be that I take your place?"

He rather hoped that Ian would say, "Aye."

"*I* fare well," answered Ian. "The grooming goes easier, now I have done it. The laird is pleased with the sagas I tell, the songs I make. Besides, Alan MacDugal, the boy you saw standing just there by me, is a friend. He hates Black Gavin even

118

as we hate him, for he killed Alan's father, as he killed ours. I teach him runic writing, and he teaches me the way the land lies; whose the land is, lying between here and the castle at Edin's Boro, where sits the King. We are friends."

"Friends," said Brus. "Have you then broken our vow? Have you told him we are two?" Brus spoke quickly, anxiously, then remembered he himself had told Gregory.

"Ssssh!" Ian warned. "Not I," he declared. "*That* I keep, as we agreed. 'Tis still our secret."

"But *I* have told," said Brus. "Gregory I must needs tell, for his help. Besides, he saw you, and would have known you are my twin. Has any time come to take the jewel?"

"Once," said Ian, "I nearly had the Black Fox."

He told Brus of the night they had ridden forth alone, of the chance he had let slip by.

"Were you daft? Why did you not kill him? *I* would have done for him!" boasted Brus. "What shall be done, then? Stay you here as before? How can the jewel be taken? Know you aught of how it can be done? Let *me* stay! I shall find a way. He should not go free had *I* such a chance!"

"Not yet," Ian said, shaking his head, "not yet, though there may be a way soon. The armorer, too, is our friend, though he knows nought of you. But he has lost all through this scheming fox; his wife and child, his home—all. He says, 'I bide.' So —I, too, say, 'I bide.' Messengers come and go. There is much secret talk; there is much lifting of drinking horns. I sing to amuse Black Gavin and his nobles. One day, there will come a time; a time when he forgets I am Norse, when he forgets he wears the talisman of Harald, whom he has slain! So—'I bide.' "

"But what of *me?*" questioned Brus. "Think you not of me?

I 'bide' also; in a shepherd's cot, I bide. 'Tis a friendly place, true enough, but it takes us not to find our mother. It lets Black Gavin bide too! How long shall he bide? If I take place here, I shall find a way soon to jerk the cloak from Black Gavin, to snatch at his lip beard, to wind his plaid around his neck and hang him by it!"

Brus ended sharply. It seemed to him that Ian was living softly, that he had found it easy to keep on in the way he had gone. It seemed, too, that since Ian had made friends with Alan, he no longer needed Brus; they were no longer like two parts of one person as before. He longed to care for the horses, to feel the weight of Duig's head on his knee. Most of all, he longed to be with Ian as they had been their lives long, each knowing the other's thought ere it had been spoken.

Ian shook his head slowly, sadly, looking into Brus's face, brown with the stain of heather.

"No," he said. "It cannot be that we change places now, for you have darkened hair and skin. It would be known. Yet, there may be a way to bring you inside the castle wall. There is a windhole opening into a passageway between stable and chapel where I tossed out the straw. It is a far drop into the wood below, but with God's help, perhaps I could draw you up the wall."

"With God's help? What mean you with this talk?" said Brus angrily. "What of the gods of our fathers? Are you gone soft, or simple?" Brus almost shouted in his anger.

"Nay, do not be angered," whispered Ian. "Sssh! Someone comes." Brus busied himself with Duig and hid his face while a carl attended the horses in the stable beyond.

"The shepherd calls you, son," the servant said, not looking up. "He's for home."

120

"Aye," Brus answered.

Ian whispered into Brus's ear.

"Look for a message on a rune stick," he said. "Look in the wood under the windhole. Look tomorrow eve. Wash the brown from your face and hair. Tomorrow eve!"

"Aye," whispered Brus, his anger flown. "Aye."

When Brus had gone with Gregory back to the shepherd's hut, Ian made plans to get him back into the castle. Between them they could better find a way of taking the jewel; a way of revenge. They could exchange places whenever it suited them; one be hidden while the other showed himself. There were passages and small chambers, stalls and byres, galleries and vaults, any number of places to hide.

First Ian must carve the message on the rune stick, give Brus time to rid himself of the brown stain. Next he must devise a way to bring him through the windhole before discovery. His eye fell on a halter hanging from a peg. It was of rawhide, tough and strong, and would support a great weight; even the weight of a well-grown boy.

Next day he collected halter lengths wherever he found them; one from each stable, not daring to take all, lest they be missed. One length of forty feet or more he found in Murdoch's shop, quite new. When the lengths were joined by safe square knots, there was enough to reach down into the wood. Pray God no guard should happen below on the road to see the leathern line dangling; no guest chance by! Ian suddenly realized upon whose help he had called. So be it! He would make the sign of the cross as well. He passed his hand over breast and forehead, though not yet did he remember the exact words he should say while doing it.

Murdoch's shop served the carpenter as well as the armorer.

Scraps of wood were easily found on which to carve the rune message. Ian was well known among the carls and liked by them. Often had he gone to the shop for bits of wood.

On the stick Ian carved out the letters in runes: "Come," and he drew the sickle moon.

It was after the supper hour, time for bedding the stallions for the night. Ian was alone in the stable.

He threw the rune stick out of the windhole.

He heard the skittering sound as it touched the wall on its way down. Then nothing more. Would Brus find it? Would it fall clear of the tree tops and land safely?

He listened, he waited—but heard nothing.

Then, from below, came the sound of the loon cry; lonely, searching.

Dare he answer? Was it Brus?

Before he dared reply to the call, Alan came in from the courtyard. Ian could do nothing. He could only hope it had been Brus's call, that Brus had found the stick and would be waiting in the wood the next night, the night of the sickle moon.

7 When Brus came to the wood and the place under
the windhole, he searched long for the rune stick
ere he found it. He turned over leaves, hunted under bracken,
and, at last, looked up into the tree above him. There it was,
caught in a high branch, the new wood gleaming white. Up
he went after it.

The stick was high enough so the branches shook when Brus put his weight upon them. He kept still for a moment and looked up to the top of the wall. There a head peered over, staring down to see what had shaken the tree.

Brus kept very quiet. Soon the guard passed on, thinking it some night bird he had seen. Brus waited till the guard passed once again. He had been wise, for the guard looked down again into the treetop, but, seeing nought, moved on his round.

Cautiously Brus let himself down from the tree, having slipped the rune stick into his belt. He waited till he was beyond the bend in the road before stepping behind a thicket to read it. It was not easy for him to read, though there was light enough. He saw the quarter moon carved beside the runic letters. That would mean tomorrow. But what were the letters before it? He wished he had learned them more thoroughly. He thought the word was 'come,' and judged what the message might be. He would go to the castle again the next night at this time. If he should be wrong, and there were no way to enter, he could still go another time.

The next night when it was time for Brus to go, the brown stain was nearly gone from his face, for Una had scrubbed it clean with ashes, and with water from the burn. She had washed his hair as well, and smoothed it with her wooden comb, standing on tiptoe to do it, for Una was a small woman. She had arranged the plaid to cover his own cloak, and reached up, kissing him lightly, gently on the cheek.

" 'Tis for good luck," she said, "and for farewell, and for thanks. 'Tis a good friend ye've been. God's grace to ye, lad, and safe journey. Take the jewel, and forget vengeance. I'll not say more. Only this: find the brother that's like ye as a twin lamb, and the two, go find the mother safe."

124

"What of the plaid?" asked Brus. "Where shall I leave it?"

"In the wood wi' the bonnet," said Una. "When dark falls, my man or I will fetch it. Farewell, lad."

That night Brus left the shepherd's cottage and went his way. Una, lying awake, put her finger to her lips and waved farewell. She wept.

The sky was clouded, the light dim when Brus made his way to the wood. No quarter moon shone, though it was the night of the quarter moon.

Brus skirted the castle wall, past the sheer drop, around the corner tower, and into the wood. He found the tree under the windhole and looked up. No rope, ladder, or handhold was there. Was this surely the night of the sickle moon? Looking about, and seeing no one, not even the guard on the wall, he gave forth a low sound; the sound of the loon's cry. He waited. He heard footsteps on the wall: the guard. The footsteps passed. He waited again; called again, his head thrown back to watch where the windhole opened, black, empty. His neck ached. Again the guard passed on his round. A bell tolled the hour. The night was darkening, the moon well hidden.

Then from the windhole a dark shadow emerged, slid down the wall where Brus could see that it was a line being payed out. Down, down the wall it came, down to the branches of the tree. It stopped. Brus began to climb the tree, first dropping off the plaid and bonnet lent him. Could he reach the wall and the hanging line? Could he get up the wall before the guard returned?

Once more the guard passed with measured tread. Brus shook not a leaf of the tree. He crept out onto a branch. Holding fast with one hand, he reached for the end of the rawhide line. It was the very end.

One hand held his weight till he could reach out with the other and swing free of the branch. He remembered the tests of weight-lifting when the youths at home had used to pull themselves up a steep cliff.

The footsteps again! Brus held his breath. They passed—he breathed again. Up he went, swiftly, cautiously, up, up. His soft leather shoes made not a sound as he touched the wall. He reached the top, was at the windhole. Footsteps again. He made himself as small as he could, hugging the ledge of the windhole, his legs entwined with the rawhide. Once more footsteps of the guard echoed on the stone as they receded.

Brus put all his strength into his two arms, drew himself in through the narrow hole, and fell into the waiting arms of his brother.

If caution had not kept them silent, breathless exertion had. Accomplishment made them jubilant, but only thumping fists and fierce handclasping could say what Brus and Ian felt at being together at last.

Brus slept beside Ian that night on the straw in the small chamber above the stable. That is, they slept when it was near to morning, for their talk wore away the night. Each had his tale to tell of all that had befallen since the day of the Pictish battle. Each could scarcely wait to tell his own, often interrupting before the other finished.

Dawn was filtering through the cracks of the wall when they came near the end of their adventures, and Ian was telling again of Murdoch Gow, who was their friend, of Alan, who needed their help, and of that night he had witnessed the secret meeting with the English.

"Why did you not take him then?" asked Brus. "*Why* let live the Fox who kills the Geese? Why do not the Geese themselves pluck out his eyes, beat him with their wings? *Why?*"

"Murdoch says there is a gathering for battle," Ian replied. "This coming and going has meaning. He says the Fox and Wolf may destroy each other with their treachery. There is turmoil in the land among the serfs and thralls. Murdoch says, 'When the pot boils, scum rises. When the scum is taken off, the good brew remains.' He says, 'I bide.' "

In the days following Brus and Ian took each his turn at being equerry. Often both were abroad in the castle at the same time, learning where passages led, what place they might find for concealment, what chance of overhearing secret plans.

They found there were deep passages below the courtyard and keep, for the castle was well founded and very strong. Stairs led off to chambers in wall and turret. Galleries wound about the hall of the keep leading to women's quarters and the master's chamber. It held nooks and crannies for hiding and for listening. There was danger that the two might be discovered, but danger had always been a part of their lives.

Once, when Alan *thought* he had just left *Ian* going into the chapel, he came upon him in the stable, his hands soiled with grooming the stallion, face wet with the sweat of effort!

His look of amazement warned Brus to think quickly.

"How came you here?" asked Alan. "By what way came you? *I* came in haste remembering my saddle girth needed stitching ere I go a-hawking. Yet, I find you here before me."

"Forget you the stair near the chapel leading to the wall?" said Brus, pointing upward to the hole in the loft chamber. "Know you not the chamber where I sleep? The one opening onto the wall walk?"

Brus knew not surely whether or no there *was* a door leading from the loft to the wall walk, nor did he know how quickly he

might have come that way from chapel door to stable. He hoped that Alan knew even less than himself!

Alan nodded slowly, gazing at Brus in puzzled fashion. "Strange," he said. "Strange."

Brus, meanwhile, turned away, lifting Alan's saddle from its hook, talking as they went, lest Alan wonder more, for Ian was ever wont to speak more often than Brus.

After that the twins were more cautious. If Ian chanced to be abroad to serve the laird, Brus kept to the chamber, except those times when none was about to see him. When it seemed safe, Brus tried his strength at wrestling with the guards. There was a hall deep in the castle beneath ground level where stores of weapons were kept, where men of the guard drilled in foul weather. There he was safe from discovery. There, too, it was safe to train Duig to instant and complete obedience. Brus taught him to come at a nod, to keep silence at the touch of his finger to lip.

If it happened that Brus served at the supper meal, or he had gone a-hunting as equerry, Ian searched out small chambers and corridors. He wanted to find a hidden way leading to those overlooking the great hall, knowing the laird's chamber must be there, for he had seen him pass the opening. In such sanctuary there was always hope of overhearing some secret plan, some opportunity for seizing the stolen jewel.

Ere each went his way, they agreed upon what time they should allow till they met again to exchange places. They judged this by various means; by the sun when it had reached a certain place in the courtyard, by the return of the hunt, or by the ringing of the chapel bell. Alan had told Ian the hours observed by the offices of the church. The bell rang eight times in the twenty-four hours, beginning at three in the morning for matins, then prime at six, tierce at nine, sext at twelve, nones at three in the afternoon, vespers at six, compline at nine, and lauds at midnight.

After compline, when most of the castle was asleep, it was quite safe for both boys to roam about so long as they kept apart and avoided the guard.

Brus and Ian each took his turn of required service that fell to him whether it pleased him or no. Each kept up practice in skills, lest muscles grow slack, eye and ear dull.

"No more may we do each other's tasks, as once we did," said Ian. " 'Tis not wise, that we know. 'Tis best for me to learn the ways of beasts, though I may never be as able as you, my brother."

" 'Tis so," answered Brus, "and I must learn the ways I lack; to be more ready with my tongue, both to speak and to sing, for I cannot always feign a hoarseness of the throat when Alan wishes me to sing with the harp. Not always will a song spring to my lips at the bidding of Black Gavin. Times, he wears not the talisman we own to goad me to fury, and without the spark of fury, there is no fire in my song."

Weeks went by. The days fell into a pattern. For most days they took turns at the grooming and serving, the rune writing and playing at draughts, as fair as might be—from ringing of prime to the sounding of lauds. They took turns going to the kitchen for porridge to break their fast or for meat and bread after nones. Each, when his turn came to go for the morning meal, carried to the other a handful of dry chopped oats, snatched from the cask as he went by. Or, when it chanced to be the supper meal, carried some part of his own, or by feigning great hunger, wheedled an extra portion from Molly the serving maid or from Ab-ghillie the cook.

130

Both Ian and Brus were in need of footgear, for long days of journeying over rough ground had worn to tatters the shoes they wore. Murdoch Gow spoke of it when he saw Ian's toe poking out.

"No man need go unshod with good tanned leather filling the shelves in the shop," he said. "Come, we shall go to work on it."

He found a suitable hide, then, taking Ian's shoe for a pattern, he cut out new ones, and showed Ian how to reinforce them on the sole with cowhide. They were made in one piece, and laced over the instep. He showed Ian how to tool the leather to decorate the sides.

"These are as fine sandals as ever I saw," he said to Murdoch as he thanked him. How could he manage a pair for Brus as well? Could he tell Murdoch?

"Ye'd be the better for a new plaid, as well," said Murdoch, looking Ian over, "and wool hosen wouldna' go amiss. Here." He took Ian into the storeroom where bolts of heavy tweed and piles of hand-knit stockings were kept for the men. When he had fitted him out, he said to Ian, "Now, ye be a proper Scot and a credit to Clan Dugal. God bless ye, lad."

'Twas near the end of summer. Heather purpled the hills. Harvest was over. Those of the clan who attended the fields came to bring the laird's measure of supply; fruits dried, or preserved with honey; wood for winter fires, sheep slaughtered, hides tanned, bolts of linen and wool. There was great brewing of ale in the alehouse and storing of it in huge vats let into the floor. Herbs hung to dry in the warmth of the kitchen, fennel, sage, marjoram, and rue; betony, figwort, lavender, and larkspur. Some were used in cooking, some for medicines. The seed of larkspur ground to a powder and mixed with vinegar was good to kill head lice. A brew of tea made from figwort was known to lift the spirits when the heart was heavy. Basil and lavender were used with other herbs and blossoms to strew bedchamber and hall for fragrance.

The smell of lavender clung to the freshly washed linen left at the door for Ian every morning. The linen was Brus's as well, but how could the laundress know that?

Jamie, the stableboy, said it was the Glaistig who secretly took away the soiled linen each night and brought it back fresh each morning.

"And who might be the 'Glaistig'?" asked Ian, for it was he who first had the pleasant service.

"She be an elf maid," said Jamie. "She do have long hair and a greenish face, and she do wear a green gown, too. She do serve the ones she chooses."

"Like the Nornir Maidens?" said Ian, doubting. " 'Tis they who bring the ale horn to the warriors. Not likely!"

"Glaistig" or serving maid, it was good to have clean linen.

There seemed no time ripe for taking the jewel, no opportunity open for taking revenge. Brus was impatient, was for action, however great the danger. Ian restrained him.

"Bide," he said. "Bide. A time will come, as Murdoch says."

Often ladies of the household appeared at table. Both Ian and Brus, when each his turn had taken, saw that Alan paid scant courtesy to Lady Julia, mother of Gavin. When there was opportunity, when Ian and Alan were together in the monk's cell, Ian spoke of it.

"Is the Lady Julia not friendly to you? Is she not your grandmother?"

"She is no more my friend than that son of hers," said Alan. "Nor is she my grandmother. She was second wife to my grandfather and is mother to Black Gavin, only, not to my father, Dugal. She likes well being mistress of Lorne. When the Lady Nineag takes over the keys of the household, she will not like it, though she must needs smile upon her at the betrothal feast."

"If she lives, where is your mother, then Alan?"

" 'Tis not known surely," answered Alan soberly. "Gavin the Black took her away, and it is thought she is in a stronghold of Dugal's near Berwick-on-Tweed, though 'tis not sure. He fears to keep her here, for these people are her friends as were they my father's friends. Black Gavin they hate for his cruelty, as do we, though which of the lairds and chieftains are for us we do not yet know. Let Gavin the Fox look to himself! A time will come, and soon, I think."

Each day when harvests were brought in a feast was spread in the court. Harvest ale went around and around. Black Gavin showed himself merry, calling for sword dance, for pipers, for singing. He lifted his drinking horn as oft as it was filled.

At times he wore the talisman of Harald, seeming to set great store by it, for it was known to be an ancient treasure. He sometimes spoke of it to guests; often smoothed it with his fingers, even as Harald had used to do. When Brus saw this, he could scarce keep his hands from it, and from seizing Gavin's throat.

When Ian served, and the laird flaunted the jewel, he, too, was driven to a fury. His fingers itched to feel Gavin's windpipe. He longed to hear Gavin beg for mercy as had the villagers whose lives he had taken.

Yet Ian made himself serve the man he hated; kept his anger within him, though nostrils flared and fiery color flushed his cheeks, remembering how Murdoch Gow had said, "I bide."

Whether Ian or Brus served him, Black Gavin seemed to

know no difference. Always he spoke slightingly to either, yet claimed often their services.

They talked out their hatred when together in the chamber over the stable, knowing themselves of too little strength or experience to carry out vengeance alone.

Once, during harvest week, three strangers came. Their speech was Southron, English, and their dress somewhat different from the Scots'. Instead of sitting at table with the harvesters in the court, the laird ordered supper to be set forth in the hall of the keep. Brus served, listening with stretched ears for any word that might fall. Ian, seeing the strangers enter the keep from where he watched through a crack of the chamber wall, went by ways he knew down winding stairs to the level below the court, then, through little-used corridors paralleling the wall, to other stairs going up again, and beyond the chapel to stairs leading aloft. There he followed a narrow passage around the upper part of the nave, and came out through a tiny doorway near Black Gavin's chamber. He hid himself behind a pillar and could look out over the hall below. He hoped to see whether Gavin wore the talisman, but little light shone into the high, arched hall. Whatever brooch he wore was hidden. Ian slipped back through the small doorway, and into the chamber where Gavin slept. He looked around. This, then, was the Fox's den! He moved swiftly lest someone surprise him. He saw a box standing on an iron bound chest. In it was a heap of chains, buckles, brooches; booty from many a conquest. He searched and searched among them, but the talisman of Harald was not there. Someday it would be there. Someday he would find it.

Back he went through the passages, seeing no one, for the household was at supper and servants busy.

It was after the bell had rung for compline that Brus came with Ian's supper. He had the remains of a haunch of mutton hidden under his tunic and an oaten cake. He had much to tell of the strangers.

"It was little of their talk I could hear," he said, "but 'Stirling' I heard, and 'the meeting of the roads'—later—I heard 'not Falkirk, but the other'—what it betokens I know not, but it is some mischief, of that I am sure."

"Aye, that I saw," said Ian, gnawing the mutton bone.

"*You* saw?" Brus lifted his eyebrows.

Then Ian told him of the way he had found to reach the upper gallery overlooking the hall. He told of the heap of bronze, silver, and gold metal ware he had found, though the brooch of Harald was not there.

"Gavin wore our father's brooch," said Brus, "and at first, I had much ado to keep my fingers busy at my task, they so ached to grasp it. Then, listening while serving kept my attention, so it was easier to forget that Gavin wore it. *When* shall we have the brooch and avenge our father? *When?*"

"When indeed," sighed Ian. "The time of ripened fruits is here. Bright leaves cover the trees, soon winter snows will fall. Yet, is our father unavenged, our mother unsought."

On the last day of harvest feasting Brus was again in attendance at the supper meal in the court. Great fires and torches glowed redly in the evening light and over all hung a blue haze of smoke. Black Gavin was jovial with new-made ale and, when he had done eating, called for a song.

"Let us hear again the fierce song of the battle with the Pictish men." He shouted, "Where is the youngling? Ee-an!"

135

Brus came from the kitchen in answer to the call. It had been long since that night of battle. He had seen that Gavin wore not the jewel of Harald this night. Could he make another fierce song?

He came forward; looked at Black Gavin, seeing his silly lip beard, knowing his vanity, remembering his cruelty.

His blood rose in answer. He was about to begin, had opened his mouth . . .

But the song was never sung.

A sudden commotion turned all faces toward the double-towered gate.

The bridge was lowered, the portcullis raised, the gate opened.

A troop of horsemen, journey-worn, clopped over the cobbles to where Black Gavin now stood awaiting them.

"Make way! Make way!" the heralds cried, sounding their trumpets. "Make way for the king's emissary!"

Everyone fell back, making a path, the servants carrying empty salvers and alepots, trenchers and ewers. There was a great din of noise; a scraping of benches, barking of hounds, ironshod feet ringing on stone, the clink of mail, the creek of leather.

Three men dismounted and approached Black Gavin, one leading.

"Gavin of Lorne," he said. "We come from Malcolm, whose oath of allegiance you have but lately taken. He commands your assistance with all your men at Edin's Boro, seven days hence, with all your forces to defend Lothian and that country between the Tees and the Tweed, against Ethelred, the Saxon King. Come you east to Stirling, where you will be joined by Rob of Clan Keith."

The company stayed not a moment to rest or take food, but went their way to gather the clans to the north.

The harvest feast was ended; swift feet sped about the courtyard. Each man went to his task at Gavin's order.

He himself went to prepare for the ride, going first to the chapel, taking Alan with him, and sending "Ian" (Brus) for his mount.

" 'Tis a brave song you'll make when this work is over," he said. "Saddle the mare as well, for ye'll go along. We've many a mile to go ere ye sing again."

Little did Black Gavin know of how many a mile! Of how far a place! Of the burden of the song Brus would sing!

There was time but for a whispered word with Ian ere Brus heard Gavin's voice calling for his horse.

"He wears not the jewel!" said Brus. "Though he may take it when he arms himself. See to it!" He sped to the ladder, let forth the stallion and the mare, then with Black Gavin, Murdoch and Jamie, Andrew Mor and Fergus Neb, he was gone; gone to gather the clans of Lorne, some to meet at Dundugal, some to meet them farther on the way to Stirling.

Out of the gate, over the drawbridge, they thundered. Then, down the steep, around by the road at the loch, through the pass, to gather the clans.

First to Canoch of Starov, then to Cambeul and to Cawdor; to Dubhglas, Dearg Comyn, to Lauman of Stalker; to Conyngam of Dunochie. All through the night, the day following, and the next night they rode, shouting the war cries, "Victory or Death," "Cruachan! Cruachan!" or "Stand Fast!" "Stand Fast!" tearing night's curtain with their shrieking, shaking the ground with wild riding.

They compassed a rough circle from Dundugal going west,

then round about and back again by Aweside, stopping only for sup and bite offered them, and to rest their mounts. The country and strongholds in nether Lorne, the long arm of land to the south, were held by another chieftain, but subject to Gavin's command.

Farmer and smithy, baker and joiner, herdsman and apothecary, all left their beds or their work, gathered what food they might; cheese, bread, a sack of oats; girded themselves with plaid and bonnet, pibroch and dirk and joined the chieftains in the wild ride.

Some came for the defense of Scotland, some for the spoil to be had, some to escape the dullness of their lives. Some came only because they feared Black Gavin. They left behind weeping womenfolk, sleeping children, desolate countryside. For when would they return? Who would tend the flocks or till the land while they were gone?

To Brus the ride through the night was almost as exciting as setting forth in the Viking ship. They forded streams, skirted lochs, thundered over hills. They dashed down steeps, rode through forest and glen. They woke the sleeping with hammering fists. Every man answered the call, either joining them on the instant or promising to follow as soon as might be.

Once, as they left Dunochie Castle, Brus found himself beside Murdoch Gow, their horses neck and neck. Brus leaned toward Murdoch to question him.

"Murdoch Gow," he said, shouting in his ear, "What think you of this gathering of the clan? Why are all ready to follow Black Gavin if he be not their proper laird? If so many be his enemy?"

"As I told ye, lad, many there be who follow wherever spoil is to be found. (Though it was Ian he had told.) And many

there be who fear Black Gavin and the chief of the isles. Many, too, would defend Lothian and take that other country, bordering, where trouble never ceases, because of the English. For it may be that *there* God will see justice done! Who knows what may happen to an unjust master on the field of battle?"

"Ah, 'tis so," said Brus, nodding his understanding. His heart lifted, for now it seemed the way was opening. A way to seize with honor the jewel of Harald and, if the gods were kind, to do away with his enemy.

Bird song greeted broad day as the horsemen, saddle-weary and hungry, neared Dundugal again.

A cloud of dust followed them. Ahead, slowly settling, was another cloud, and through it, now and then, could be seen another company.

"Canoch of Starov, it must be," cried Gavin, putting spur to horse. He shot forward, shouting again the war cry.

"Victory or death! Victory or death!"

The company ahead raised the cry: *"A-gael! A-gael!"* halting, while Gavin Dhu thrust forward at a gallop. So—it was not Canoch of Starov but Bègan Mòr who was ahead. Gavin drew up to where Bègan awaited him, and, without more than a brief greeting, dashed on, leading both columns, around the bend of the road at the base of the castle, and on up, up the steep to the gate.

The drawbridge was lowered at his command, and all entered the courtyard, where Gavin then dismounted beside Bègan.

Alighting, nearby, was Bègan's daughter, the Lady Nineag, with her servant, Jenny.

"God's grace to you, sir," was Black Gavin's greeting. "And to you, Nineag the Fair. Have you then been warned of Malcolm's order?"

"Bègan Mòr waits not for order!" was his reply. "Malcolm himself has but late been to Glenelg, where I met him, and with Rob of Clan Keith, we pledged the chiefs thereabout at the *mod,* the clan gathering, and there we parted, he to go toward Edin's Boro and I here, for Nineag's sake, and to rest horse and man ere we ride on."

"Shall our house be honored then with the Lady Nineag's company whilst warriors go to battle." Gavin bowed low to the girl Nineag.

Brus, seeing the quick change in Gavin from brutal warrior to sleek courtier, wondered again at his wiliness.

"He can in one moment be fierce as a cornered fox, and in the next, smooth as clotted cream," he thought. "But the maid Nineag *is* fair; fair enough to gentle any beast," he concluded as Ian had done, long ago.

Where was Ian? Had he kept to the chamber? He must have done, else someone would have seen him and known they were two, for all had seen Brus leave with Black Gavin to

140

gather the clan. He must wait to find Ian till the laird's mount had been tended.

Horses were led to the far end of the courtyard, for there was no room in the stables. There they were tethered, fed, and bedded, for on the morrow they must ride forth again.

Bègan and other masters of clans who had joined Gavin's company went with the womenfolk into the keep. Great preparations went forward to provide food for the considerable number of men and horses gathered into the castle yard. Beside the nobles there were stableboys and grooms, equerries attending the chiefs. When Brus had tended Gavin's mount, he made no bones about going straight up to the chamber, and there found Ian, who was peering out of the narrow slit to see what went forward below.

"So—you are back," he said to Brus, half resentfully, for the nights had been long and the day endless, cooped in the small chamber. But as the hours had gone on their slow-footed way, he had news to tell. Waiting had worn away its edge, as long use wore the edge on a belt knife.

"Aye, back," said Brus, excitement still showing in his brightened eye, his quickened breath. "How fared you? Stayed you here, in this hole?"

"Here, most times," said Ian. "Though I went after lauds to the chapel to say a prayer for our mother and for you, and——"

"A *prayer*? For *me*? Are you daft? I can take care of myself, and the gods be kind. I need not chapel prayers! Come, how go we now? Do you stay here, and I go? Or go we both? 'Tis a man's work we are on. Yet—leave you here I must not, for we are as one in our purpose."

Ian looked sidelong at Brus. Should he tell his news? Brus seemed to have taken a high hand. Let him wait a bit.

"What of Alan?" he asked. "Goes he with Black Gavin? I saw him not in the courtyard. And shall we keep to revenge?"

"*Not keep to revenge, say you?* What manner of son avenges not his father" demanded Brus. "In heat of battle, the hawks of Harald shall avenge him!"

"And what of this Alan. This harp player, this son of Clan Dugal? Is it *his* twin you are? Or mine?" Brus suddenly grasped Ian's shoulder in his strong grip, pinching into the flesh. "And what of fair Nineag? Perhaps you would stay to defend *her*!— Would you? Coward! Lilywhite!"

But already Ian's fingers had found Brus's throat.

"Call you *me* coward? Say you *I* am traitor?" Ian clutched Brus's wind pipe so his breath whistled.

For a moment they struggled, each against the other in bitter enmity. Body strained against body, arm against arm, fierce fingers biting cruelly into flesh. Suddenly blue eye looked into blue eye, each seeing himself mirrored there. Ian slackened his grip. Brus loosed his hold. Arms slipped around shoulders. Embrace took the place of struggle, laughter the place of scowl. They rocked with it. Ian recovered first.

"The news!" he cried. "The news I have! I near forgot." He fumbled through the things in his purse, bringing out the tinderbox, the amber piece, saying meanwhile, "I followed that secret way, in dead of night, whilst all slept, round about below, then up and through the gallery." He handed Brus something wrapped in a scrap of old linen. "When I heard the snoring of the guard, I went to Gavin's chamber. I could tell by the feel it was the jewel, though little light——" Ian stopped speaking, for the look on Brus's face was not the look of joy he had expected. "What?" he said. "What is wrong? Are you not rejoiced that it is ours once more?"

"But 'tis *not* ours," said Brus sadly. "This is some other stolen treasure. See you here." Brus pointed out the setting of the stones. "Here is no magic rune such as Harald's has. It is like, very like, but 'tis not ours."

"You are right," said Ian. "I had forgot. This seemed to be the talisman, and I had forgot the magic rune. Now what shall be done? It will be missed as the jewel of Harald would have been."

Brus and Ian both kept silence, thinking. Then, said Ian:

"I know of a way. Whilst you tend the laird's mount, can you not 'find' this in his harness? As if Black Gavin had caught it and it had dropped?"

"But where," puzzled Brus. "It must be somewhere that it could have been lost for some time, lest he suspect, for had it fallen from his plaid, the plaid would be unfastened."

"Could it be found in the hall as if had caught on his tunic, his sleeve?"

"Aye," said Brus. "That will do it. Give it to me, and when the time is right I shall return it. But it must be soon, lest he find it gone. I must watch and be ready."

"Aye, ready," answered Ian. "'Tis readiness that counts most, as our father said."

"Stay you here," said Brus, "whilst I bring food. I am famished. So must you be. First, I must attend the Fox at table. Let us hope he has not looked for the jewel. 'Tis likely not, for he means to set forth at tomorrow's dawn for Stirling, and is occupied with making ready. I shall see Murdoch Gow. He *must* know we are two. We must tell him our secret. He will find cover for one of us. Stay you here till I come."

"Aye," said Ian. "I'll bide still."

Brus went down to the stable where Duig jumped to meet

144

him, barking his joy, as they crossed the courtyard to the big kitchen, he found Murdoch finishing his porridge. Only Molly was near, filling Murdoch's bag with oatmeal from the great cask standing by. She greeted Brus and went to the fire to fetch his breakfast and dish of scraps for the hound.

"Whissst!" said Brus into Murdoch's ear. "Know you of a plaid can be had for a boy to keep us company?"

"A boy?" questioned Murdoch teasingly. "A plaid? What like kind of a lad would it be now, who has no plaid of his own?" Murdoch wiped his mouth with the back of his hand, speaking behind it.

"A lad like me," said Brus. "*Just* like me; so like, he comes and goes in my stead, and nobody the wiser." Brus looked sidewise at Murdoch to see if he understood.

"Aaah, aye," said Murdoch. " 'Tis just as I thought, there be two of ye! He nodded his head up and down.

Even though he had expected Murdoch to guess he and Ian were two, he drew back in surprise. He had thought no one knew. Not even Murdoch Gow!

"Aye," said Murdoch again. " 'Tis the way ye have with the beasts that told me. I've said nought, so the secret be safe wi' me. These be times when one man tells nought to another till he be sure where friends lie. Be ye *Ian* or the other?"

"The other, Brus," he whispered as Molly set the bowl of porridge before him.

"The one knowing the way of the beasts," agreed Murdoch. " 'Tis not much difference I see between ye, but difference there is. The wolfhound never follows Ian about as he does you. That I've ever noticed. There'll be a plaid and a bonnet in the stable for the lad Ian," he promised, "and 'twill match your own."

"And shoes," said Brus, lifting his foot. "These we share, but no longer may we share them. Ian's fall from his feet. Will there be time? Can I make another pair, think you, this one day?"

"It can be managed," said Murdoch. "Much have I to do with harness and chain mail, but come to the shop and there I can give you help to make the shoon yourself. Plain they must needs be, for there is no time for tooling, but they will serve.

"Make haste now, lad, and give a hand where 'tis needed. The laird must be ready for the road, the morn, and none delay, else it be *himself* that does it! Nineag the Fair would be cause for any man to delay." Murdoch went out laughing.

And so it was. Sumpter horses, laden with gear, (tents, food such as might be carried) and men-at-arms in ring mail, carrying spear and battle-ax, claymore and dirk; farmers and herdsmen with bow and arrow; all stood, waiting and ready in the cold dawn, half the hour while Black Gavin stood in the garden with the Lady Nineag, saying farewell, she, drawing slowly away toward the door of the keep as if more than ready to leave. He, loath to go, armed cap to toe, lip beard sleek, gauntlet off, saying last soft words.

Ian could see them from the passageway where he waited till the last moment to join the company, the warm plaid around him, the bonnet covering his hair, new shoes on his feet, his face smeared and darkened. He carried the bow of yew Murdoch had made him and arrows slung across his back like one of the foot warriors.

He went to the other side of the passage where he could see through a peephole into the court. He would mingle with Bègan's men till they were out of the castle and on their way.

After, he would follow, hidden as before. In the confusion of starting off no one would notice whether he be of Bègan's men or Gavin's. He carried the tinderbox and the amber piece, some bread, and a handful of oatmeal brought by Brus.

Among the horsemen he saw Alan. How he wished Alan might go too.

He went again to where he could look down to the garden. He could see the lovely Nineag standing by the fuchsia bush, and Black Gavin, one hand on his great sword, the other smoothing his lip beard. From below, in the courtyard, came the sound of impatient stamping of hoofs, shuffling of feet. When would the farewell be said?

Then it was over.

The Lady Nineag slipped through the door and was gone. Gavin went out by the arched gate to the courtyard, blustering as he went, for haste.

"To horse!" he cried. "To horse! Eee-an! My horse!"

"Here, sir," answered Brus, who stood near the double-towered gate, the stallion at the ready, his own mount at hand. Swift as thought every man was mounted, every foot warrior alert. Then a shout went up, and from every man's throat, the war cry.

> "A-gael! A-gael!"
> "Stand fast! Stand fast, stand fast!"
> "Victory or death! Victory or death!"

Through the gate and over the drawbridge the cavalcade poured forth, pennants waving, men shouting. Hounds followed, baying, while Ian joined those at the end of the procession, those afoot.

When the gates had closed behind him, Ian drew a deep breath of thankfulness.

He was free!

8 Brus, too, felt the thrill of freedom. He rode near
Black Gavin for any service he might give. Near
enough to hear some of the conversation between Gavin and
Bègan Mòr, for, being kin, in a sense, they rode together. The
lesser chieftains and their men rode in separate companies as
they joined the column.

Brus heard a word now and then—Lothian—Ethelred—Northumbria—earldom.

A gesture—toward the south—toward the north.

A laugh—a smirk.

More words—Malcolm—Abington—Falkirk.

A leaning from one to the other.

Bègan's equerry rode near as well. Could he guess at what went forward? Or did he *know?*

Did the two ahead think Brus deafened by pounding hoofs? Or did they think him stupid as he knew they thought Murdoch Gow? Little knew they how well Murdoch had schooled him in the way the land lay. What plot was between them Brus could only guess. What this scheming had to do with the English who came that time to Dundugal he did not know. Something—of that he was sure. He must find out how they matched.

He wondered whether Ian had come safely through the gate. Would they meet at nightfall? Would they meet at all? He searched in his purse for the brooch Ian had taken for Harald's, to make sure it was safe. How could he return it before Gavin missed it? Then he thought, "When we make camp, and while I stow Gavin's gear, I shall slip it in among his things and say nought. Let him guess how it came there."

Where the road from the north came through Strathfillan and toward Crianlaruch they were joined by Canoch and his men. The company was now nearly a thousand strong. Brus could not help considering each chieftain as he joined them. Which were for Malcolm, as all were supposed to be? Were Bègan Mòr and Gavin going to the support of Malcolm? Or were they hoping for the victory of Ethelred the Saxon?

He could come to but one conclusion. *They were for Bègan Mòr and for Gavin.* Each for himself alone. *Alone—all one.*

Brus remembered how his father had always said, "Search for a man's weakness, and when you have found it, he is yours." Gavin's weakness was vanity, surely. Another was greed. That weakness Bègan Mòr had as well. Big as he was, and as his name, Mòr, implied, and standing well above every man in his company, greed could be his downfall. Brus recalled another saying of his father's. "The greater a man's greed, the smaller his size."

Somehow these failings must be made to serve a good purpose. He would think on it.

Now that the company was complete except for Clan Keith and those others to be met at Stirling, the cavalcade moved at a faster pace. Pipers tuned up, and after the first whining sounds played so lively an air that even those reluctant to leave home showed their excitement in quickened step. Brus, too, felt his blood run swifter at the ancient call to battle, and wondered if Ian felt it, and whether it had kindled anew his purpose. "One who hears the pibroch must be stirred to action, for 'tis hair-raising and skin-tingling, the sound of it," he thought.

The way led over hills and through mountain passes, through vale and forest.

They camped that first night in a vale among the hills. Each company had its own camp, its own cook fires. Some hunted in the forest for fallow deer and wild pig. The hounds ran down wolves, and brought down foxes. Brus sought out Murdoch Gow to tell him of what he had overheard, but there were no means of getting his ear alone. The nobles plied him with gear and armor to be repaired. Ian, too, was occupied with tasks among Bègan's men, and only by looks one to the other could he and Brus speak.

Simplicity and hardness of living gave these warriors strength and endurance. Their way of life was not strange to Brus or Ian. Skin of deer in the form of a bag was used as cooking pot, and hung loosely on stakes over a fire. Spits were used by some instead, and meat was roasted, the spits resting on piled stones. Besides meat, oatmeal was cooked, which every man carried in a bag. Water was found in many streams, running pure and free down the hillsides. It was mixed with the meal to form a paste which was then cooked on iron plates carried by the sumpter horses among the gear, or carried by the foot warriors, each his own.

In the busyness of making camp Brus found it easy to return the brooch Ian had mistaken for Harald's. He saw Ian among the foot soldiers, but just long enough for one to glimpse the other.

Two nights more the warriors camped, going on through the day till dusk fell. The men cared for the beasts, ate what they carried in their sacks, and slept where they fell, so wearied were they. There was no chance for Brus to speak to Ian, nor had he the will or strength to search out Murdoch Gow. "I'll bide," he thought, "till we get to Stirling."

All the day following the warriors came through a vale into low country bordering the River Forth. By early afternoon the fortress of Stirling came into view. It rose on rock sheer against the sky, a powerful fortress, which it needs must be, for here many roads met. To the west were the hills, the slopes deeply forested. Giant oaks marched down to the river's edge, spreading moss-covered roots to trip the unwary. There, on the level ground, Gavin halted the company.

"Here shall we camp this night!" declared Gavin as the horsemen filtered through the forest to the open space which lay below the castle. "Here shall we find meat and sport to our liking. When the men with the camping gear come up and fires are made, we shall have deer, wild pig, pigeon, and fat grouse to cook. Come, youngling, take from me these gauntlets, this shield. Lighten my load, for 'tis heavy." He smoothed his dark locks, ran his fingers over his lip beard.

Brus stowed the heavy gear beside a tree, putting the laird's ensign beside it to show where it stood. The other nobles, too, divested themselves of helmet and shield. The hounds, Duig and the others, sensing a chase, leaped and yelped, running about, urging their masters on. Bows and arrows were unsheathed, spears lifted, men remounted, and they were off, spreading through the forest, each man for himself.

Brus kept his horse near to Gavin's, and soon they were out of sight of the others. Only a faint belling of hounds reached them, telling of quarry sighted, game taken.

For an instant, quite near, an antlered stag stood above the bracken, then bounded away. Gavin threw his spear, but missed. When he had recovered it, he was off after the leaping stag, through dead fern and tangled thicket, Brus close behind, and Duig far ahead, baying.

In and out among the brush and trees, over root and stone they rode, the deer ever just ahead, but moving branches showing the way. Brus saw the stag leap a small stream and vanish. He saw Duig, too, cross the stream, then stand with puzzled look, while Gavin dashed through the brake.

Then, a stumble of Gavin's mount, a crash, and Gavin pitched headlong onto a stone, his head under water.

He lay still.

Without a moment's delay Brus leaped from his horse and came up to him. He struggled to lift Gavin from the water and up the bank, then recalled *who* and *what* was Gavin of Lorne!

This man was his enemy! This Gavin Dhu, this Fox, murderer of fathers, killer of children!

Brus almost let Gavin drop back into the stream. Who would know he could have been saved? Let him drown!

Yet—leave him to drown he could not. Something inside Brus compelled him to bring Gavin to safety and to seek the place where the hurt was. A lump was beginning to swell, but no blood flowed. Gavin was but stunned, and soon began to turn his head.

Brus, when he saw Gavin recovering consciousness, moved away, attending the horses, calling Duig, giving no sign by word or look that he had saved Gavin's life.

Gavin, if he remembered the fall, gave no sign either, though his wet plaid and soaking, aching head must have told him what had occurred.

But was he not Gavin of Lorne? Was he not the best horseman in the West Country? Vanity would not allow him to admit owing his life to a mere boy, a boy who was his captive.

"Come," he said, "we've lost the stag, and I have lost my taste for sport this day." He painfully mounted, motioning Brus to follow.

Brus wondered why he had troubled to save him. Yet, save him he had, surely. Then, he seemed to hear his father's voice, as clearly as if he had really spoken, saying, "—and be just to all men."

But was it "just" to save the life of an enemy? "Yes," Murdoch Gow said. "Love thine enemy, hate him not, but hate the thing he does." Was he, then, becoming soft like Ian? He must watch lest he forget his purpose.

They found their way back to camp, where now the foot warriors with the camp gear straggled in, and the hunters came

154

back by twos and threes, bringing enough meat for the supper meal, and more than enough.

Brus, as they rode out of the trees, began to whistle a folk tune known to Ian and himself from the old time. He slowed his going, hoping to see Ian among those afoot.

There he was. Brus saw him lift his head at the sound of the whistling, not too quickly lest someone see, rather a stretching of the neck, a tilting of the head as was their wont to do. It was enough. Ian was among them.

That night, when camp was being made, monks came from a nearby monastery, going among the men to hearten them, to say the office, to offer prayers for the King and for Scotland. They brought casks of ale of their own brew strapped to the horses' rumps, and were promised payment for it after victory.

Brus saw that one of the monks, Brother Michael, talked for some time with Gavin of Lorne. When the monks were ready to return to the monastery, Gavin summoned Brus.

"Hey, cockerel," he commanded Brus, "go you with this good brother and bring back the bundle of new-made bread he will give into your care. Bring it to *me,* mind ye, not to Ab-Ghillie the cook. 'Tis not for the men, but for me. Mind!"

To the monk he said, with a wry smile, "New-baked, Brother Michael, and enough to last till we get to *Fawkirk.* There, we fast till the King meets us with the other forces. Perhaps he will meet us next morn. But till he comes, we fast." He seemed to make a point of the fasting, to show that the church at Falkirk had some significance to the men who heard him speaking.

"Mind, Ian, bring it to *me,*" he said, waving Brus off.

Brus was loath to leave the camp, for the smell of boiling venison, roasting hare and grouse fair pained him, he was so hungered.

As they moved away from camp, Brother Michael said:

"Gavin of Lorne kens well the ways of battle and strategy, though the ways of peace are yet strange to him and to these borders. Let us pray the Almighty this plan for Scotland works well, then in this wilderness there shall yet be a highway for our God."

Exactly what plan Brother Michael thought it Brus could not know, but one thing he knew. It did *not* favor Scotland. It was for Ethelred the Saxon, or, rather, for Gavin of Lorne.

They rode up through the wood to the priory, where a porter opened the door to them. Brother Michael showed Brus into the sanctuary and asked him to wait, slipping the covering from his head, saying:

"The place where men meet to seek the highest is holy ground, my son."

Brus felt a warm tide of red creeping over him, because he had lacked courtesy. Though this chapel was bare and austere, it was the sacred place of the priory, even as the great hall in Trondhjeim was the sacred place of the Norsemen. Harald, his father, had told about that wonderful hall, describing the carven beams overlaid with gold leaf, the carven doorways and lintels, with the magic symbols weaving in and out of the fabled animals. Yet this place, too, though so bare and clean with its stone walls and dark beams, its thatched roof, and echoing floor, seemed to hold a quiet peace. The broken figure hanging from the rood above the altar held Brus's gaze. This, then, was that Christ of whom he heard so much, who had given His life for His friends. He had been a noble warrior.

A bell rang for vespers, and a procession of monks filed into the sanctuary, chanting as they came, each man passing Brus without a glance, his thought only upon the words he chanted:

156

" 'I will lift up mine eyes unto the hills, whence cometh my help. My help cometh from the Lord. . . .' "

"The words are true," thought Brus, his mind going swiftly to the hills of his native land, then back to this Scotland, where he now was. His thought flew to that morning when he had stood beside his father, his death so hard to bear. He had looked to the hills, and had been comforted.

When the monk came for him, Brus took the bundle, wordless, but as he rode back to camp, he thought on the monk's parting blessing:

"He that dwelleth in the secret place of the Most High shall abide under the shadow of the Almighty—there shall no evil befall thee—only with thine eyes shalt thou behold and see the reward of the wicked. . . ."

Had the blessing aught to do with Gavin the Black? Had it aught to do with him, Brus?

When the bundle had been delivered and Brus was unsaddling his horse, he saw that the belly strap was almost worn through. He took it to Murdoch Gow for mending, and while they worked together, he told Murdoch of his errand to the priory for the bundle of bread, and told him all he had heard as he followed close to Gavin and Bègan Mòr; the mention of Lothian—of the Saxon king—of Falkirk, of Abington.

"Aye, 'tis sense it makes," said Murdoch. "Fawkirk lies below Stirling as I told ye. 'Tis on the road to Edin's Boro. Abington Cross lies below still farther and can be reached by another way. 'Tis plain Gavin Dhu means to go on to Abington and give the lie to what he tells his men. That 'bread' will be a monk's robe for his disguise, for he means to be a pilgrim going to Abington Cross, there to meet the English.

"Aye, that'll be it." He nodded. "Abington Cross. Watch and

listen, lad, for we must know when. They must be caught at the very moment when the deed is done, else we have no proof. 'Tis only suspect without proof. Whate'er ye hear, tell only me. For only with greatest care may we outwit the sly fox, Gavin.''

Brus promised. Then he said, "Know you the sound of the nightjar?''

"Who knows not that tiresome sound,'' answered Murdoch, "though I've heard it not of late. Why?''

"For this,'' said Brus, "it is a cry we use, my brother and I, when we are in need of finding each other in dark of night. We cry it only twice, whereas the creature itself gives forth the cry endlessly. If you should hear it—twice—very low, know you that what we suspect is true. It may be no time will allow me to see or tell you. If twice you hear the cry, then twice again soon after, that will be Ian. If I learn that Gavin leaves at dawn, I will cry out once more.'' Brus softly gave the signal to Murdoch: "Wheep-or-wheel, wheep-or-wheel!''

"I shall have my ear tuned for it,'' agreed Murdoch. "My hand on't, and God's blessing. Twice, you say?''

"Aye, twice,'' said Brus, "then again twice Ian answering, and *still* again twice if Gavin goes at dawn.''

Ian, who was still camping among Bègan's men, saw Brus come riding back from the priory. He would wait till dark, then go to him somehow. First he would make some sign. Meantime, like Brus, he was ready for food.

While the feasting was at its height, the camp most noisy with laughter, singing, and piping, new figures came through the wooded vale to join the company: the men of Clan Keith. Some were horsed, some afoot. Like the others, all were in battle dress. Place was made for them near to Bègan's men.

It chanced that Ian was welcomed among them, for he made himself useful, lending his tinderbox to light their fires, offering to help them skin a deer, little as he liked it.

While among these strangers Ian was slow to speak and of few words, remembering the old saying, "Great babbling turns to ill for one who speaks to a cold-ribbed man." And who could tell which of these men was warmhearted?

Like the wise old owl of the forest, he heard more than he spoke. And, like Brus, he heard enough to be sure that Bègan Mòr and Gavin of Lorne planned some treachery. He strained to catch what was being said, for the words of Keith's men rolled strangely, and accents fell oddly to his ear.

One fellow, scraping away the deerskin with his belt knife, said quietly to another, one being Bègan's man, the other Rob Keith's, " 'Tis here at Stirling, the roads bear south. One, d'ye see, goes to *Fawkirk,* the left." (For that is the way he said "Falkirk.") "There," he went on, "the men do march in the morn, to meet Malcolm's men, for 'tis at Fawkirk the road bears left again and goes on to Edin's Boro. But, d'ye mind, there's another road leads out on the right to Bride's Brig, and on to *Abington.* I heard the whisper of it. *Abington!*" He stopped a moment to look around, then went on again, softly, thinking nought of Ian, who kept his fingers busy and his eyes on his work. "—Rob Keith, d'ye ken, falls in wi' the plan to give over Malcolm to the English, he having no love for Malcolm, but secretly, he watches Bègan Mòr. Well he knows that Bègan, the greedy wolf, thinks to devour Rob's own country, Caith Ness, and knows Bègan wouldna' hesitate a moment to give over Rob Keith, if it gained him Caith Ness, that north country, or to betray Gavin Dhu if it brought him the country of Lorne."

"Aye," said the other fellow, "I've thought it mysel', though I heard nought. 'Tis the way of them that has, to take more, be it Gavin of Lorne, or Bègan the Big."

"Here is treachery within treason," thought Ian. "Bègan Mòr means to be false to Gavin as well as to Malcolm and to Rob Keith." He wanted so much to find Brus and Murdoch Gow and tell what he had heard he could scarce stick to his task to the finish, though he made himself do it. He *must* find Brus. He hadn't seen him for two days, except afar off. He would wait.

Later, when alecups had been drained, and singing and laughter had gone out of the men, Ian was still awake, waiting to make sure all slept.

Suddenly he heard a wolf's howl, long, lonely, frightening. Could it be Brus, signaling?

But the sounds following, which was their signal, came not. He remembered having passsed under ash trees as they marched, remembered the silvery bark, the yellowing leaves.

The wolf howled again. Every hound in the camp barked, answering the challenge. Warriors here and there roused for a moment, then dropped back into sleep.

Once more the wolf howled, but farther off. Was he under an ash tree? Did it portend evil for Gavin of Lorne, who held the talisman? It was a gruesome sound in the night. If that blood-chilling sound woke not the warriors, what would? He would go in search of Brus, now!

"With God's help," thought Ian, "Gavin shall fall into our hands, and soon!"

The men about him slumbered on, sleep-thralled. Sleep on, warriors, sleep on, Gavin. Seldom a sleeping fox gets a goose-bone, or a sleeping man victory.

Ian looked about once more, making sure none feigned sleep, then rose without sound, and went toward the part of the wood where Gavin's company lay.

He heard the nightjar's cry—heard it twice.

He answered—answered twice.

When he had answered the cry of the nightjar, Ian heard it once more, but once only. Had that third cry any meaning? He waited a moment, but, hearing nothing further, went toward Brus. It had surely been his signal. What noise his going made could have been night sounds of small animals seeking food; rustling leaf, crackling twig, snuffling breath. These sounds men knew of old, and heard them not in sleep, so careful going roused no warriors, alerted no sentries.

The sentries, posted one to a company, weary with marching, warm with food and drink, stood leaning wherever they might lean, against tree, against rock, unknowing. Ian crept around them, one after the other, through the murk, for a heavy mist lay over the land.

Brus, too, that same night had heard more of the treasonous matter. Black Gavin and Bègan Mòr sat together at meat. Bègan Mòr proposed that they use his drinking horn and make a wager between them who could empty it most often. Gavin matched Bègan, draught for draught, from the great gold-rimmed horn. Brus filled it over and over again from the casks the monks had brought. Laughter had risen, pibrochs screeched, singing had run through the camp.

When tongues are loosened, words escape the leash of the mind.

Brus heard Gavin say, "Before dawn, I ride." He raised the horn to drink but found it empty. "More ale!" he cried. "More!"

162

When Brus told him there was but little left, he paid no heed, but cried again for more.

"Finish it off!" he cried. "We shall be thirst-quenched this night. No one knows what another night will bring! Finish it off, I tell you! Take the ewer, eaglet, and draw off the last of it." Brus went off, thinking to himself, "Little you know what another night may bring: how the eaglet can fly, nor how loud he shall scream!"

He opened the tap of the cask.

Out came a leak—an ooze—a drop—a trickle—the cask had run dry.

"You've come to a drought, guzzlers!" Brus said to himself. He took this time to find Murdoch, but he found him not. He carved a collop of venison from the joint, and filled his oatmeal sack thinking, "No one knows when he may need food."

When Brus returned with the empty ewer, he found Gavin snoring, mouth open, lip beard awry, feet sprawled, arms slack.

Bègan Mòr slept as soundly, the last of the ale spilled over him where the drinking horn had dropped. Brus looked about him at the whole sleeping company. Softly he said:

"Ye be all dream-thralled, your senses given up to the god of sleep. Even the wolf's howl woke ye not, though three times it came chilling from the hills."

Brus had wondered briefly what the wolf's howl portended, when he had heard it, but his whole mind was given to Black Gavin, lying there, so vulnerable, sleep-stolen.

Sudden excitement sent new life through his tired body, for there he saw on Gavin's shoulder, winking in the fire ember, the stolen jewel. It had been hidden before in a fold of the plaid.

With shaking hand he slipped the pin from the cloth and

moved away, backing slowly, slowly till he could whisper to Duig to follow and to be quiet.

He sat down among the sleeping warriors to make sure he had not been seen, and to consider what next to do.

"How easy it would be," he thought, "to plunge a dirk into Gavin's heart! How easy to have done with it!" But he shrank from killing a sleeping man. Caution, too, told him he knew not which of these men he might trust, save only Murdoch, and he was far to the rear. Where was Ian? He *must* find him. Dare he whistle? They must get away to warn Malcolm before it was too late. He could now let Murdoch Gow know their suspicion was well founded. He would risk it.

He whistled: "Wheep-or-wheel! Wheep-or-wheel!" not too loudly, but clear and true. He listened. Then it came; Ian's reply: "Wheep-or-wheel, wheep-or-wheel!" Ian was not far off. Once more he whistled as he had promised Murdoch to do.

In a moment Ian emerged from behind an oak, a darker shadow in shadow.

Then Ian saw Brus. He was sitting, only a dark shape, but unmistakable, one hand to ear, listening, one upon Duig's head. Suddenly, when a twig snapped under Ian's tread, Brus rose, followed by the hound, and came toward him, stepping among the men. Duig, too, stepping delicately, made no sound.

When they came near to each other, Brus motioned Ian to an opening in the wood where faint light showed a thinning of the trees. With one accord they moved toward it, scarce breathing, holding their plaids close and, avoiding the sentry, and going out of the wood where bushes screened them.

No sooner were they beyond the edge of camp than they began to speak and to compare what each had heard, Brus keeping his hand on Duig's head for silence.

164

"What know you?" asked Ian. "Heard you aught of their plot? Bègan's men and Rob Keith's spoke in whispers near me, but 'twas loud as a trumpet to my ears. The English are to be at Abington Cross. Know you this?"

"This I know, and more," said Brus. "Gavin rides at dawn to Falkirk, where Gavin *says* he goes ahead of them to prepare himself in *prayer and fasting!* The bundle brought by me from the priory is not bread as he claims, 'tis a monk's robe to hide him as he goes forth from the camp at dawn, to pass the sentries, and lest he be seen at Abington." Brus searched through his purse. "Look you here!" he whispered, though, dark as it was, nothing could be seen. He thrust into Ian's hand the jewel of Harald, guiding his fingers around the magic symbol. "See?" said Brus. "The other had not this."

" 'Tis wondrous, having it once more," said Ian, "but what now? What will chance when Gavin finds it gone? And if he has it not, will the magic work evil for him? I heard a wolf's howl. Heard you?"

"Aye," said Brus. "I heard it. But magic or no, Gavin Dhu of Lorne shall soon meet evil. Come, we must get on!"

Ere they could move, the shadow of a man stood over them. Fear had scarce begun to stiffen them when they were reassured. The man was Murdoch Gow.

He motioned them farther away from camp, and all three dropped to their knees, creeping over hummocky ground, sometimes marshy and wet, often scratchy with thistle and brier, Duig loping along behind them. When they were well away and near where the horses were tethered, they stopped for breath.

"Ahhh!" said Murdoch. "My knees are overstiff for crawling, but 'tis good to breathe free! Now, let us consider what ye do."

166

They stood in the murk of night, even now keeping voices low.

"We go to the King," said Brus. "This matter is for his ears. Gavin of Lorne rides at dawn to Abington, there to meet that English noble who came to the castle." He began to loose the horse tethered near to that of Gavin.

"Aye, to the King," Ian echoed. "I, too, heard of matters that should reach the King's ear. Now, it seems we be Scots, for young Alan MacDugal needs our aid, and he is Malcolm's man." Ian related all that had passed between Bègan Mòr's man and Rob Keith's while they worked together. " 'Tis truth as we said, Murdoch Gow, the Wolf will eat the Fox! Bègan Mòr plans treachery not only to Malcolm, but to Gavin of Lorne as well!

"Come, let us begone, Brus, else the Fox will get away!" He made as if to mount, but Murdoch stayed him.

"Soft, soft!" he cautioned. " 'Twill never do for ye both to go! Gavin will be warned and we shall not catch him at his evil deed. One of ye must bide and the other go. Which shall it be? In this glower, I no can tell which from t'other, but one must bide."

" 'Tis best for me to go, think you?" said Brus, beginning to mount. "I had thought we two could go and be free of this murderer, and bring help to wreak vengeance on him."

"Aye, to be free of him and his commands seems too great a boon to give over," said Ian, "but I see 'tis best for one to stay. If I be the one, how shall I answer Gavin when he finds the talisman gone? And if you ride off, how shall I tell him the reason my mount is gone?"

"Aye, the lad speaks truth—*Ian* be ye? The way ye handle yon beast, Brus, and the way the hound sticks close, tells me now which is t'other," said Murdoch Gow.

"This now is my counsel. 'Tis best for all to be as it was when sleep took Gavin. The brooch *must be returned,* else he may suspect he is discovered in his treason. Do not fear, it shall be yours when all's done. Trust old Murdoch, and trust in God."

He laid a hand on each boy's shoulder. "How are thy shanks? Good for walking?"

"Aye, we cover ground well, as we proved when we came from the Winged Isle," said Ian.

"Aye, good," said Brus. "If walk we must. But I am more sure with a belt knife, should enemies be met. And Duig answers my every nod. Let *me* be the one to go."

"Ye must decide for yerselves," said Murdoch, "but 'tis Brus that's best wi' the beasts, 'tis Brus has been attending Gavin this journey, 'tis Brus that should bide, say I."

"So be it," said Brus, though unwillingly. "I'll bide."

"Ye'll mind how I said, 'The Lord has His own way of vengeance,' " Murdoch went on. " 'Tis not lads should take it into their own hands. Come, down off the animal, my lad. Say farewell one to the other."

Brus dismounted and gave Ian the food he had.

"Ian, be ye on yer way," said Murdoch. "But first, be sure ye *know* the way to Edin's Boro." He turned to Ian, mapping with finger on open palm, describing the way the hills were set.

"The road is just here beyond the fen, then go ye south by east," he said, "keeping the high ground aye on the right— so. The river widens here and flows into the firth. A few hours walking will bring ye to Fawkirk, ye'll know it by the stone chapel there. At Fawkirk, the road goes east, and ye'll know by the cauld wind that blows straight off the North Sea on yer left. Keep straight on to Edin's Boro. Ye'll pass a castle, but say ye are for Malcolm and ye'll no be stopped.

168

"Time passes. God save ye now, and God save Scotland. Stay!" he said sharply. "Ye must know, Ian, that some there be among the nobles that are for Malcolm; *most* of them. Give ye that message to the King. But he has need to know how things stand, and to be at hand. Fare ye well!" Murdoch grasped Ian's shoulder, and took him by the hand. He made the sign of blessing and farewell.

Ian, crossing himself, said, "God be with you, brother," embraced him, and they parted.

9 When Ian's form had melted into the misty dark,
Brus and Murdoch went back across the fen to the
sleeping camp.

"We must make haste," Murdoch said; "there is much to be
done. We must make sure that the Fox does not go to ground.
He must be taken. I shall rouse those chieftains I know to be

Malcolm's men; Canoch, Conyngam, Lauman; these I am sure of. The others, they will know. Go ye now to Gavin, and put back the brooch, ere his sleep begins to thin. He must think all's well when he wakes. Bègan Mòr has his own eels to fry. Watch him. Rob Keith will likely see to him. 'Twas not for nought, Keith went up to Glenelg. We *must* get to Abington before Gavin Dhu. He shall be shorn of his name and title, and his power for evil. God's grace on ye, lad, till we meet at Abington."

They parted at the edge of the wooded camp.

Ian, leaving Brus captive still, set his face south after finding the road above the fen. It was easy to keep his direction, even in fog, for Murdoch had said that ever at this time of year the wind was wont to blow from the northeast and it had the chill of the North Sea in it. Besides the moon shone pale and illumined the fog.

To the right high land rose, like that on which the castle stood.

Where Ian's path was the going was easy and he made good speed.

"Pray God I have many miles behind me ere Gavin wakes from his stupor," he thought. "With Christ's help, I shall make as good distance as he, though he be horsed and I go by my long legs." He held the amber token, smoothing it. It was a comforting keepsake.

He breathed deeply and lengthened his stride. Times the fog lifted, times it grew so thick he must slow his going to keep to the track, for in places the watery swamp came close on either side. He kept to a rhythm in his walking as he had been taught. "Rhythm in walking aids ground covering, and eases muscle, as rhythm in words comforts the mind, aids memory," Harald had said.

Long before dawn Ian reached the small village of Falkirk. When he came to the stone church, he went in. "I shall say a prayer to God for the safety of our mother, and for success in our undertaking."

A vigil light burned on the altar, lighting up the rood which hung over it, Ian thought again how like the amber token was to the cross, though one arm be short. "It *shall* be a cross! No more shall I call it 'Thor's hammer.' " He rose and went on his way, keeping the token with its new name in his hand. He swung again into the rhythmic walk. When he passed early wayfarers, he kept his plaid over his chin, grunted, "Good morrow," and hastened on. As he left the village behind, the bell on the peak of the church rang the hour of prime. Now he knew the hour, and he knew the way.

He began to be hungry, and when smoke from cook fires and smell of porridge came from village cottages, they raised a storm in his middle. He took out the piece of venison and chewed on it, and later ate of the meal he carried. It somewhat stilled the tiger of hunger that was in him. He kept to the long rhythmic strides and covered the ground swiftly. The fog burned off and the sun shone, somewhat tempering the cold wind.

By midday the dark stone of Linlithgow rose in sight, lying below the rise of ground where Ian was. Would he be challenged? Who kept the castle? Who was kept prisoner here?

The road lay close to the castle wall, and, skirting it, went on past to Edin's Boro.

"What manner of answer shall I give should the wall sentry stop me," Ian wondered. "Shall I say I am of Clan Dugal? For so I am, being friend to Alan, who is true master of the clan. God willing, this day's work may give back his birthright. Aye, I *am* Dugal's man!"

He wished Alan had been with him. What good company they would have made. Then he wished it had been Brus instead. The two together, free, on their way to find what had befallen their mother and the others. Alan was overyoung for adventure, and had not had Harald to train and harden him. Alan was not ready.

Ian came under the castle wall.

"Who goes on the King's highway? Who trespasses on Lothian soil?" bawled the sentry from the watchtower.

"A man of Clan Dugal!" shouted Ian. "With an urgent message for the King!"

"Pass!" said the sentry. Ian went on.

"Four hours' journey from Castle Linlithgow to Edin's Boro, Murdoch said," thought Ian. "Now I am more than halfway."

By late afternoon the ground rose to many hills again, and Ian knew from what he had learned of Alan and from what Murdoch had told him that he was near to his journey's end. Soon he could see, high on a rocky hill, stark and strong, the fortress of Edin's Boro.

There were ravines to cross, hills to skirt, the village to pass; a village of narrow wynds and closes. Then Ian was climbing the steep way, which still wound, up and up, to the outer castle gate. There the sentry stopped him.

"What do ye here, lad? This be a fortress, not a school for pink-cheeked boys! What do ye here?" He stood with spear across the gate, barring the way, for all that he laughed at Ian's youth.

"I be of Clan Dugal," said Ian with dignity. "I bring urgent news to King Malcolm. Open! Make haste! I have come all the way from Stirling. Make haste!"

"What can ye show that ye be Christian? Ye do have a strange sound to yer tongue. Be ye Saxon, now? Or *Dane*? What can ye show?"

"I be Scot, now," said Ian instantly. "Look!" He thrust the amber token under the sentry's eyes, holding it so the short side of the crosspiece was hidden.

"Ah, the cross!" said the sentry, dropping his pikestaff. "Pass, friend!" He opened the small door in the great gate, and as Ian passed through, shouted to the inner gateman, *"Open! Open to a man of Clan Dugal! A message for the King!"*

Ian clasped the token more tightly. This cross must be a good talisman indeed!

As he climbed the long ascent to the level courtyard, each sentry from gate to keep bawled in his turn the order to let Ian pass.

He was taken into the hall of the keep, and told to wait.

The hall was much like that of Dundugal, but larger, and covering one wall was a hanging of embroidered cloth showing a hunting scene—men, animals, birds, flowers, and grass. It was a marvel to look upon. As Ian gazed at it, he saw it move.

His eyes were drawn to the side where the hanging was being lifted.

It was being lifted into folds, folds held back by a hand, a lady's hand, for it was smaller than a man's and more shapely. Ian saw the shine of a bracelet above the hand, a bracelet of twisted silver, and even without being able to see it clearly he

knew the *bracelet was finished at the opening with carved sheepsheads!*

On indrawn breath he said, "A-a-a-ah!"

For Ian knew that bracelet, or one like it. He had cut his teeth on it.

Passing the hand which still held up the arras in folds, a tall woman entered—the Queen—Ian knew it must be the Queen, for she wore a golden circlet on her head. She was followed by the other woman, and the arras dropped into place.

As Ian waited for her to come into view, he kept a startled silence and stillness for fear he might be wrong, not even looking at the queen, but standing, open mouthed, staring at her woman in waiting.

A cry, from Ian or from the woman in waiting, or from both;

175

who could tell? And the two fell into each other's arms. Ian had found his mother—Ragnhild, her son.

"Where?" asked Ragnhild. "Where is your father? Where is Brus?"

"Our father sleeps with the heroes," said Ian. "Brus awaits me with the clans——"

The Queen spoke.

"A new day has come, indeed, when the Queen takes second place after her lady in waiting," she said imperiously.

Ian immediately dropped to his knees before the Queen, asking pardon for unseemly neglect of his obligation to her. Ragnhild, too, knelt before the Queen, saying:

"Your Majesty, only I can know your goodness, who have been near to you these many weeks since our ships foundered here and all who were saved, captured. Be gracious still, and forgive this, my son, and me also. Seeing him is like to seeing one who has been to the Hall of the Slain, where indeed their father, my husband, now is."

"Though Queen I am, a queen may take what place she chooses, and now I choose second place." The Queen smiled graciously, bidding Ian and Ragnhild to rise. "To see a smile on Ragnhild's face, I would gladly wait for homage and to give you my welcome." She stretched out her hand.

"The King will receive you, but even now, he readies himself to set forth, and there is need for haste. A sudden illness of mine, from which I am now recovered, had delayed him, else he had been gone, for he meets the clans at Falkirk. Come, we shall await him here."

"But no! Your Majesty," Ian exclaimed. "He must go to Abington! That is why I have come to him. To warn him!"

"Peace!" said the Queen. "You shall tell him." She moved

176

toward the fire and motioned for Ragnhild to sit beside her on a stool, as was fitting. Ian stood. There was so much to be said and told he could not speak at all, but must stand with tears coursing down his cheeks. Their mother was found!

"Who shall speak first?" asked the Queen. "Ragnhild, tell your son, which is he, Jan or Brus? I know they are twins, as like as two sprigs of heather, for I have heard you say so."

But Ragnhild could no longer hold back the questions on her tongue. What had become of Harald? What of Brus? How fared the warriors and the ship?

So Ian must tell his side first—how ill fortune had followed the *Raven* and all who were in her, save only himself and Brus, who served King Malcolm by staying to watch Gavin of Lorne.

"But your father," begged Ragnhild through her weeping. "Tell me—how came he to die? He was of a strong race, and a valiant warrior—how was it with him?"

Ian, holding his mother close, retold what he knew and what he had heard from Brus, describing as well as he could the place and the cavern where their father lay.

When she could speak, Ragnhild said, touching her forehead and breast in the sign of the cross, "God's will be done."

"*God's* will?" questioned Ian with a startled, joyous look. "Then you too are Christian?"

"Aye, Christian, though I learn but slowly," agreed Ragnhild, "and bear my cross unwillingly. But these noble captors have persuaded me by their mercy. And you, my son? How is it with you? Follow you the Christ also?"

"Christ's way seems good to me," said Ian. "Besides, I have a friend, Alan MacDugal, who has taught me in the way of it. But Brus will not heed. He will not give up vengeance. He likes it not when I speak of Christ's way, so I say little of it to him.

177

Now, because you and I accept it, it may be that Brus will follow."

Then suddenly Ian rose, remembering again the need for haste. But ere he spoke, the King himself strode into the hall. He was accoutered for battle, in chain mail, his shield and sword borne by an equerry, banners carried by pages. He was followed by masters of clans of eastern provinces and highlands; MacBane, Davidson, and Robertson from beyond the Tay, MacDuff of Fife, Ramsay and Lindsay of East Lothian, and Hay from Berwick-on-Tweed.

When the King heard Ian's story, how Gavin of Lorne was on his way alone to Abington Cross to meet the English, he said:

"Now clears the tangle I long have tried to unwind. 'Twas for this I went to Glenelg and met Bègan Mòr of the Isles and Rob of Clan Keith, yet I cleared it not. You say Gavin left for Abington at dawn?"

"So he said he would do," said Ian. "Though he was so sleep-stolen he may sleep still."

"We shall go by the shorter way and reach Abington before him, with God's help."

Already the King had turned toward the Queen, embraced her, speaking as he went toward the door.

"Come, lad," he said. "I shall learn more as we go, and the name you wear. Come!"

A quick farewell to Ragnhild, an obeisance to the Queen, and Ian was following the King's company. In the courtyard he was horsed and mounted like the others and placed beside the King's equerry.

With a wild cry—*"For King and for Scotland!"*—they were off, clattering down the sharp slope of the cliff, down, down, into the ravine and across to the other side. Then, up again to higher ground, going south this time on the highroad to meet the road from Stirling at Abington Cross.

First rode the heralds, carrying banners and swords, then the pipers, pibrochs slung over shoulders, fringed plaids flying. The King and his nobles came next, followed by the equerries, Ian among them. Then the whole company of liege lords and their men. The pace they rode was as if they had been flying, for it seemed to Ian that hoofs scarce touched the ground, that horse and man were one, and they rode the wind, for it was in their favor.

There had been no time for grief at parting with his mother again, no time for the food he had so much needed, and there was no thought of it now. Excitement filled him.

Through the Pentland Hills they rode, skirting the heights, pounding through glens. They crossed bridges, forded streams, charged through villages.

Into the night they rode, a full moon giving light all the way.

When it was needful to slow their going, the King called for Ian to draw nearer that he might question him.

"Come forward, lad," he said, "and first tell me your name, for I know it not, though Ragnhild, your mother, has been for some time in the Queen's service, and I know her story. Tell me, how came you to the country of Lorne?"

"*I* am Ian, Harald Redbeard's son, and my twin brother is Brus. It is he who is now with Gavin of Lorne. When our ship, the *Raven,* was wrecked on the Winged Isle, Bègan Mòr took me prisoner, because it chanced that he found me first when I got water to drink from the burn on Bègan's land. He commanded our men, those left, to attend with our father, Harald, the betrothal feast of Gavin Dhu and Nineag the Fair. When one of our men, Birger Harelip, lost his temper and attacked one of Bègan's men, the whole feast turned into a battle. All our men were killed and thrown over the wall for dead. But my father still lived. Brus found him and saved him. Later, when Brus had gone for water, someone came to the cavern where he lay and killed him, and stole the jewel he wore. We now know it was Gavin of Lorne, for he is so vain that he wears the brooch openly and taunts us with being orphaned." Ian sighed.

"You tell a lucid tale, my son—Ian, did you say?"

"I am Ian, sire. Brus could tell the tale better than I, for he it was who kept hidden outside the castle and found our father."

The ground now leveled; they could resume speed. With a gesture of acknowledgment the King pulled ahead and they were off again at a gallop, raising the war cry:

"For King and for Scotland!" Every man took up the cry till it echoed over the hills.

Murdoch and Brus, after seeing Ian off, each going his own way to perform his own task, slipped back into camp. Brus carefully put the brooch into a fold of Gavin's plaid. He neither moved nor stirred, nor did Bègan Mòr, but slept on as if death had taken them already.

Brus settled himself with Duig close for warmth, and began his vigil. He saw Murdoch's shadowy figure step among the sleeping warriors; saw other figures rise and move off; saw them loose the horses tethered in the open space, and one by one, lead them quietly away. Duig trembled and started to whine, but Brus's touch stilled him. He heard the pounding of hoofs in the distance as the mounted chieftains reached the road and went off. They would surely be there at Abington Cross to take Gavin the Blackhearted when he arrived to meet the English!

Gavin and Bègan Mòr slept on. Brus rubbed his eyes to keep awake. Sometimes a sleeper snored or groaned; sometimes a sentry came enough awake to pace a few rounds; the wolf howled again. Brus wrapped his plaid closer against the chill.

Then the great body of Bègan Mòr began to move; he sat up, shook his big head; stood to his tremendous height. Brus, watching from under his plaid, saw him going clumsily through trees, over roots, around sleeping men, yet without rousing a single warrior.

He had not gone far when a succession of small sounds caught Brus's attention. Bègan seemed not to notice, but moved toward the open space. Brus threw off his plaid and rose to see what went toward. Commanding Duig to stay, he followed and hid behind a tree where he saw, but was not seen.

As Bègan Mòr stepped into the open place, he was seized. He made not a sound, for a heavy plaid was thrown around his head. Four clansmen carried him to the center of the space. In silence, except for the straining and grunting of the men who bore him, he was brought to earth with a war club. The clansmen stood off, raising arms in triumph, yet keeping silence, still. It was awesome. One moment Bègan Mòr was alive, walking; the next he was gone. Where? To the Hall of the Slain? But that was the place of heroes. Where?

Brus watched to see what disposal the clansmen would make of Bègan's body. They made none. They left him where he had fallen, and went away, out through the other side of the wood.

Brus crept back to his place near Gavin. It was near to morning. Would Gavin wake?

Brus settled himself again beside Duig. Would this night never end?

The fog began to seem whiter than before, its chill more penetrating. Then Brus could distinguish the faces of the warriors about him. Should he wake Gavin? No! Never! Let him wake as late as he would; the more time for Ian to accomplish his errand, the more time for the clan chieftains to arrive before him at Abington Cross.

Dawn was sifting through the trees when Gavin stirred and woke, looking still dream-stolen, thought Brus. Gavin looked about him, then seeing the bundle of "bread," remembered, rose swiftly, and when Brus started to follow, said, speaking below his breath.

"Come you, then? I thought to go alone to make my communion, but come; 'tis a long ride to Falkirk. Make haste, the dawn is already clearing the mist. Leave the hound," Gavin tossed over his shoulder.

Brus, knowing Duig's obedience, shouted, "Back!" *but motioned him to follow!*

Brus followed quickly, with Duig at his heels, skipped across the hummocks of the fen and had loosed the horses by the time Gavin reached them. Gavin stopped to undo his bundle of "bread," and as he got into the monk's habit it contained, gave Brus a wry smirk, handing him his plaid and bonnet to tie behind the saddle. Brus said nought, but with a shrug handed Gavin the reins, and himself mounted the other horse.

Up to the road they went, then, Duig racing beside Brus, galloped the mile or two to the fork, where the road divided, a sign pointing one way to Falkirk, the other to Bride's Brig.

"*This* road! To the right!" shouted Gavin, leading the way. As Brus knew, *this* was the way to Abington Cross.

If he made no remark, Gavin might suspect him of knowing more than he said, so Brus asked the reason for going right when the sign read "left."

"Someone's tampered with the sign," said Gavin, and Brus nodded as if he had agreed.

Skirting the hills that rose steeply to the right, Brus followed as Gavin urged his mount to swifter and swifter pace. Duig kept close behind, for this chase suited him well. Never did he go to Gavin. After several hours' riding they came to a wide river and stopped to rest and water the horses. Duig kept close to Brus's side, and obeyed his every command, but kept free of Gavin.

Gavin had little to say except: "The hound, I said, was to be left," but when he moved toward Duig, the beast bared his teeth, and growled. Gavin, feigning not to notice, said:

"Come, 'tis well on into morning, and 'tis a long way still to Falkirk." He mounted and they crossed the wooden bridge where two rivers met, skirting the rocky fortress, and into more level country again.

On and on they rode, and for hours the road was over low ground. They came in sight of the river again and crossed a branch of it, fording the stream.

By now it was well into afternoon. Brus was very hungry and wished he had cut a second collop of venison to keep for himself. He wished, too, that the bundle had been really bread from the monks' bakery, instead of the cowled robe that Gavin wore. There was no sign of the clan chieftains, who had surely passed this way long, long before.

They came to a village, and Gavin, because of his monk's habit, and that he said he was on a pilgrimage, was given bread and cheese, and a mug of ale at the small inn, the "Sign of the

Thistle," which he grudgingly shared with Brus. The horses were fed and watered, and a bone thrown to Duig.

"Wasting food on a beast," said Gavin. "He should have been left, as I said."

"He followed," said Brus, "and 'twould have wasted time to take him back."

Gavin only tossed his head, mounted, and motioned Brus on.

When they left the village, the way began to rise into the hills. It slowed their going, and the horses began to tire, breathing heavily.

"Stop we must," said Gavin, dismounting, "else the mounts will not hold out to Falkirk. Rub them dry, Ian, and walk them to cool their blood." He sat himself down on a stone.

How far beyond stood Abington Cross? Brus could not tell. He began to think and remembered that Murdoch had said, "Near to fifty miles to Abington Cross from Stirling." They had been riding since early morning. They had been slowed by streams, by wooded land, and by hilly ground. Perhaps Abington Cross was still far away. Would the nobles be waiting? What would happen? He rubbed the stallion's coat with a clump of grass, wiping away the sweat, then dried the mare's coat as well, and walked the horses up and down the roadway.

When Gavin rose to mount, Brus tightened the saddle girth.

The leathern strap that had been mended was worn nearly through again. Would it hold? Should he leave it? If it broke, Gavin might be plunged from his horse; might be thrown over a cliff. Something Brus could not explain made him fix it.

Dusk had fallen, he could not see, but let his hands remember the way, fastening the girth with the buckle tongue thrust into a hole made with his belt knife.

He mounted and they rode on. Mist wavered over the low

184

places among the hills. The moon rose. They threaded their way through a thick forest, crossed a river, and beyond, Brus saw the stone church, the cross in the square and the clustered houses of the village. No man was in sight, though a faint light showed in a cottage.

Where were the chieftains?

Gavin spoke.

"Here be our journey's end," he said. "Stay you here outside the church. I have need for being alone at my devotions."

"Devotions," thought Brus. "I know your devotion!"

He waited, holding the horses, every muscle tense, wondering where Murdoch Gow could be, what plan he had followed with the chieftains. He thought of Ian and wished they had been together. Was that a horse tethered at the wood's edge? He could not tell.

For long Brus waited, sitting on a stone marker. Duig whined; Brus stilled him and drew him close for comfort. Excitement of waiting for he knew not what set his teeth chattering.

The light in the cottage grew more dim; the night more and more cold.

He heard hoofbeats; they came close.

A man rode up from across the square; by his look the same Englishman he had served at Dundugal. He came to the church and went inside, not seeing Brus in the shadow.

Almost instantly there arose a great clamor, shouts, curses, a bursting forth of heavy bodies.

Brus saw Gavin and that other, held fast and being thrust forward by men he knew. Others ran forth from the wood, from the village house nearby. Brus saw them gather, saw torches begin to flare.

Duig pulled at his hand, dashed from him yelping. Brus ran after him to the cross in the square. He must see what was taking place.

A company of horsemen thundered over the bridge.

It was scarce morning when Ian with the King's company neared the meeting of the roads, but Abington Cross stood dark and clear in sight, for a ring of torches lit the scene. Horses and men milled about a central figure. Whose they could only guess, for it was hidden by those around him and the murky light.

"Some have an urgency to catch the Fox of Lorne greater than the King's. They have beaten us to the kill," said Malcolm as they slackened speed.

He dismounted, taking his claymore from the herald, moving forward with the others to where the knot of people was. Shouts and curses covered the sound of their footsteps till they were very close, Ian being nearest the King.

Malcolm parted the company with raised sword and command.

"Make way!" he thundered.

The crowd separated, revealing the figure in the center. The Fox had been run to earth.

It was Gavin Dhu of Lorne. He was caught, held fast by his own men. They had ripped off the monk's robe and he stood in tunic and breacan, his arms pinned back, prisoned by the iron grip of Conyngam of Dunochie and Lauman of Stalker, one at each side. Nearby stood Brus, who stepped toward Ian and grasped his hand. Gavin looked beaten, done for. Yet his eyes opened in astonishment when he saw the twin brothers standing together.

He looked again at Brus.

186

"So," he said bitterly, "ye are twain; two cockerels from a double-yoked egg."

Beside Gavin, held prisoner as well, was the Englishman who had been at Dundugal. Surrounding both were the clan chieftains, rounded that night they had gathered the clans. Ian remembered them all; Canoch of Starov, Cambeul, Cawdor, Dhubglas, Conyngam. Beside Brus stood Murdoch Gow.

"GAVIN OF LORNE," roared the King, "there is but one end for treachery! The sight of you sickens me! Take him away! Men of Lorne, deal with him!"

He was led aside. Brus and Ian saw the flash of a blade, heard a thud. It was the end. Harald was avenged.

The King addressed the Englishman.

"As for you, my lord, snake of the border, never has sword dipped so willingly into Southron blood." There was a "whhi-i-p!" of sound from the King's claymore and the Englishman fell.

There followed a council of the nobles to decide the next move.

Murdoch Gow came to Brus and Ian, taking their hands.

"A good job, well done, lads," he said. "Ye were ready for the doing of it. 'Tis readiness that counts. God has given us a true leader at last in King Malcolm. Ye be avenged of yer father's death, yet, yer hands are clean. Here, as I promised, is the brooch of Harald, your father. Which of you shall have it? Which of you is first-born?"

"Brus is first-born," said Ian. "He shall have it. And if he wills, I shall keep the token I now call a cross, though 'tis Thor's hammer in our country."

"Aye," agreed Brus. "I am first-born, so our mother has told us. The amber token that was given me by Sigurd shall now be yours, Ian. 'Twas to be for the one who traveled alone, and 'twas you who went alone to the King, my brother."

"And now all's square," said Murdoch. "God's blessing on't, and go ye to find the mother."

"But I've found our mother!" cried Ian. "Brus, Brus, this matter did take it from my mind, 'twas all so hasty!"

"But where, *where?*" cried Brus. "Where is our mother—how was she saved? Oh, now indeed God has blessed us!" He ended thankfully, not aware of his saying it.

Ian rushed on. "Mind you the bracelet our mother wore? The one she says we cut our teeth on?"

"Aye, I mind," said Brus waiting, "Go on, go *on!*"

"I saw a lady's hand holding back the wall hanging as I waited for the king. On the wrist was a bracelet, a bracelet I *knew*. I held my breath in fear I was mistaken. The Queen came under the hanging, and following her—our mother. She attends the Queen and was saved by her. She awaits us even now!"

"Our mother!" said Brus again. "Our mother!"

"But there is still work to do," said Ian. "Alan's mother is still prisoned. We must find her."

"Aye," said Brus. "You are right; there is still work to do. But we shall find her."

The council ended. The King turned to Brus and Ian, and Murdoch bade them farewell.

The King spoke.

"Those who defend our throne and person, our land and country, shall not find Malcolm lacking in gratitude," he said, wiping his sword with a kerchief as he spoke. "Have you aught of favor to ask, either of you? Your mother will, of course, be restored to you."

"I have a favor, sire," said Ian. "Shall Alan MacDugal be master of Lorne as is his right? Shall his mother be released from wherever she may be?"

"My hand on it!" said the King, grasping first Ian's hand, then Brus's. Then he bade them kneel.

He touched each lightly on the left shoulder with his great sword, saying:

"I, Malcolm, do claim allegiance of you, as you have already proven. For service to Malcolm and to Scotland, I pledge to you Brus and Ian MacHarald, my protection and my trust. Do give you lands and men once held by Bègan Mòr, which shall be yours, equally, and your heirs. Bègan Mòr met the death he deserved, for traitor he was, and blackhearted as the one who now lies yonder, slain. I now know what long I suspected.

"His daughter, fair Nineag, shall be under the care of Clan Dugal, and of the mother of Alan Ban. That other mother of Gavin the Black, shall be taken and prisoned. Go you now back to Edin's Boro. You are overyoung for battle, and that needs must follow. But God has given us the advantage through you and we shall win! God speed you!"

As they rode away from the crossroad, Ian took from his purse the little amulet of amber.

"See," he said, drawing his horse level with Brus's, " 'tis a cross, though 'twas called Thor's Hammer."

"Aye," agreed Brus, "A cross. I see 'tis."

"The cross took me into the castle of Edin's Boro, and our mother made the sign when I left her."

"Our mother too?" said Brus thoughtfully. " 'Tis a good sign. Let us follow it, for now, WE BE SCOTS!"